WOODARGON

BY

STEPHEN HOLMES

PublishAmerica
Baltimore

© 2004 by Stephen Holmes.
All rights reserved. No part of this book may be reproduced, stored in a retrieval system or transmitted in any form or by any means without the prior written permission of the publishers, except by a reviewer who may quote brief passages in a review to be printed in a newspaper, magazine or journal.

First printing

ISBN: 1-4137-3331-X
PUBLISHED BY PUBLISHAMERICA, LLLP
www.publishamerica.com
Baltimore

Printed in the United States of America

Dedication

This story is dedicated to my grandson
Stephen and to all the women in my life.

Wife..........Patricia
Daughter..........Gillian
Mother..........Edith

To my cousin –
Jean and the Morrison family.
Read in good health.
Stephen.

WOODARGON

Robert Wilson – The last Woodargon
Roxelena – Heir to the throne
Peter Foster – Robert's friend
Robin Hood – 2nd Woodargon
John Little – Robin's friend
The Scarlet – Son of Will Scarlet
Pook – Hobgoblin / Fairy
The Bishop - Vargis
The Sheriff – The black death
The tree people – Children of Robins band
Sayer of soothes – Visionary
Sayer of soothes wife
Mam – Mother
Dad – Michael
Mr. Alritage – Teacher
Mr. Travis – Teacher
David – Peters brother
Teddy Lambert – Bully
King John – The pretender
King Richard
Queen Elena
The Sorcerors
Lorben – The 1st Woodargon
Margola – Robin's sister
The kings guard
The Sheriff's soldiers
The villagers

PREFACE

You are invited to enter into a world beyond reason, for this is a tale of a young lad and his friend whose thirst for adventure becomes more than they bargained for.

This medieval prophecy is fulfilled when time brings back the last "Woodargon" (keeper of the forests and sanctuary below). These settings take place in the sprawling woodlands of Yorkshire, England, in 1247 A.D.

A journey like no other was about to unfold for Robert Wilson and his friend, Peter Foster. It all began with the discovery of a grave site that would forever change their lives as they are plunged back into the pages of history to face a test beyond their wildest dreams.

Now in another time, they must seek out their destiny and fight the good fight against tyranny to restore the crown of England to its true heir. It is a time of magic with heroes, heroines, and villains all mixed with unforgettable characters who bring the story to life.

THE INFANT YEARS

Over the years the pages of time have been kind and turned with a relative ease for me, but this year's celebration will be sadly remembered alone, for my dearest friend Peter has passed away some six months ago.

Once again July 25th has arrived to remind me of the great adventure that Peter and I were part of fifty-four years ago. I am now in my seventieth year and live a contented life with my wife, daughter and grandson – Stephen.

I have often been referred to as a quiet man, and although words dance merrily in my head, they stubbornly refuse to tumble with purpose from my tongue, and so with a greater ease, I put them to paper.

To start my journey, I must go back to the very beginning. Robert Wilson is my name. I was the only child to father Michael and mother Edith. I was born in the town of Uddersfeld, Yorkshire, England, during the winter month of December 1941. I came into a world of turmoil with a global conflict of man determined and succeeding in reducing his population.

My parents were labeled ordinary people from the working classes of northern England, but on reflection, I consider they were extraordinary with strength of character and a tenacious will to survive and prosper. The class system in Britain consisted of three distinct levels. One was represented by the wealthy and politically affluent upper classes. Many of them believed they were superior in every respect to all living things. Then emerged the middle classes from which many longingly considered that they rightfully belonged also in that upper class fraternity. Finally, there were the lower classes, which made do with, among other things, servicing the other two classes. Although now greatly diluted, this system strongly represented a discriminatory who's who in the regime of its time.

During the early war years we lived in a row house in Mike's home city of Middlesbrough, a port and shipping centre located on the north east coast of England. It was definitely on Hitler's bombing "hit list." Row houses were aptly named for their structure of multiple living units being joined end on end, which gave the appearance of one long horizontal building with a plethora of doors, windows, and chimneys, so that the term "living beside each other" was truly and geographically realized.

From my entry into the world I was easily identified by a birthmark of a small, but perfectly shaped oak tree, brownish in color, located in the heart area. It became, in my mind, a boring point of discussion in the early years, but its relevance in the course of time would be revealed.

As an infant I remembered the nights being loud and eventful because of the bombing raids. People would congregate in air raid shelters wearing government issued gas masks, and I would still cringe at the memory of a strong rubber odor, which they emanated. The masses would habitually drink tea and sing songs of happier times, yet in spite of the hazards and hardships of war, I believe these island people were a hardy lot brought together by a kinder, caring spirit that would be difficult to find today.

The days, well, the days just seemed ordinary. My strongest visual memory during those early years was that across the street from our house, there was a large building, which I later discovered to be a church, had one morning simply disappeared. Although I could not verbalize the sight on seeing the one remaining wall, a picture depicting the cause of its destruction came into my head, and all was revealed. This was the beginning of events that, although natural to my being, would challenge the very laws of nature.

Memories of my father were few except that he was in the army and away at war much of the time. Then in 1943 the news came that he was missing in action on the beaches at Dunkirk, France. His death was confirmed six months later.

Mike was a steel worker on the docks of Middlesborough. The work appeared to be hereditary as he, his father, and other family members were also steel workers. I believe their philosophy in life was: work hard equals play hard. It was said that Mike certainly appeared to fit into that mold. If he had lived, I often wondered what affect as a role model this man would have had on my own life, but it was not to be.

In the course of time my mother finally made the decision to move back to our hometown of Uddersfeld, where there were friends and relatives, and so preparations were in the making. The day of our journey was set, but Mam decided to reschedule to the following day, as she had a dream of a train disaster with some casualties. This vision of doom indeed came about for as we discovered the following day. A number of people had been killed in a train mishap while on route from Middlesbrough to Leeds, but for us fate had been kind. Now, Mam and I were alone with only two bags and the clothes on our backs, yet I felt a calm reassurance on our arrival to Uddersfeld. Even as a small child I had a feeling of familiarity and a comfort that I somehow knew of this place and had been here before.

It was not easy for my mother to become a single parent during a time of great hardships. I can only describe her as a very determined just "get on with it" kind of woman. She had an amazing capacity for simplifying life, and although she was not well educated, her common-sense approach to our survival was ever present.

The insanity of war was now coming to a close and with it post-war Britain began its slow recovery. Life at that time was more than challenging, but Mam was a soldier and a survivor in her own right. She gained employment in one of the many cotton mills of the north, where she and many others did backbreaking work for little pay, but continued with bravado and always a song or two. On occasion, during those early morning rituals I recall watching her as she prepared to do battle with the day ahead while friends cared for me. We would say our farewells with a kiss after which I would run to the front room window where a silent goodbye was sealed with a wave that perhaps lasted a little longer than it should. I watched as she slowly disappeared into that early morning fog while crossing that familiar cobblestone street. For a number of years, I remember that day after day, she wore the same work clothes – A well-worn long heavy gray woolen coat that disguised a washed out and faded pinafore beneath, along with a head turban that an Arab would be puzzled but ultimately impressed by. The workers as they were labeled would march toward the sound of an early morning siren that enticed its congregation to begin the hardships of a Mill day.

We lived in one all-purpose room of a large boarding house, which many others occupied, all sharing a single outside backyard toilet. You could tell the destination of an occupant by their purposeful steps towards the rear of the house along with that carefully folded newspaper tucked beneath one arm.

I've always chuckled at the dual purpose of a newspaper, which at that time provided information, etc. during the visit, and then, of course, its ultimate use and disposal.

A Childhood of Discovery

I was now four years old and my association with school was about to begin. On that first day, Mam took me by the hand and promptly walked me about a mile to my new school. On arrival, I was puzzled by the sight of so many yelling and running aimlessly. Being an only child, I was used to my own company and far less pandemonium. I suppose in retrospect I was simply considered, and indeed was, a quiet lad.

It was quickly decided that my first public school day was not to my liking. After all, I didn't know anyone, and nobody seemed particularly interested in me. During play time while in the school yard, I thought, "Well, that's enough for one day; it's time to go home." As today, I had an amazing visual for directions. Once I had been somewhere, I could return with ease. Anyway, on my appearance Mam gave a stern warning that I remain in school until its days end, and she took me back the following day with an explanation that meant little to the headmaster who was in charge and quick to let all know it. Among other things this man was short in stature, and I suspect more aware of it than anyone else. Also he was fashion conscious and meticulous about his attire, usually overdressed, which perhaps in his mind made up for his physical shortcoming, and so the focus of his day became a fixation for both appearance and authority, ensuring that everyone was well aware that he was completely in charge.

I soon discovered the power that teachers seemed to enjoy over their pupils, with discipline being a daily priority, and I often became aware of their unpredictable moods.

P.T. (physical training) was for me a time of escape and self-expression with sporting events such as football, cricket, and swimming high on my list. Then boxing became part of the curriculum, which I did not like. It emphasized physical domination of one over another. While I was not considered an aggressive boxer, I could certainly look after myself when it became necessary. To my dismay, I was selected for the school boxing team, and I recall on one occasion being paired against Teddy Lambert, the school's best boxer and worst bully. He was, of course, the aggressor in our duel, but I was able to anticipate his every move until a girl watching our battle shouted something that momentarily distracted me. As I foolishly turned in her direction, Teddy delivered a low blow, which both winded and angered me. Moments later, when I had somewhat recuperated, our smiling coach allowed the duel to continue, perhaps anticipating more of what had just happened, but my aggression had now been aroused to the point of completely dominating my opponent. A very surprised Teddy and an even more surprised teacher quickly stopped the bout. In retrospect, I must admit I was a little disappointed with my uncontrolled reaction to the low blow.

I had now reached the age of ten and although my life seemed pretty normal up to now, I soon began to realize that there were forces at work, which were beyond my control or understanding.

It all started with Mr. Travis who was in charge of P.T. He had what we referred to as the torture cupboard, which contained a variety of instruments for inflicting pain that I'm sure Mr. Travis relished in the dispensing of. He was easily identified by the daily wearing of a black suit which imprisoned the nauseous smell of moth balls that followed him everywhere. He was a man of absolutes, for if nominated the guilty party that was enough to pass his usual verdict, and its consequence. Mr. Travis would order you to meet him at the cupboard, which was strategically placed facing the class. At that time he would open it to display a ghastly selection of canes and straps hanging there. We also noticed an old spiked running shoe hanging from one hook, which I believe was displayed for affect rather than use. At least I never saw or heard of it being used. Mr. Travis would then ask you to choose the instrument for your punishment, as if your part in this activity would somehow justify the event. Then he would eagerly proceed with the execution of it. This scenario was repeated on a regular basis, yet only once to me, and thereafter, never again. Predictably I was nominated and found guilty of a trumped-up charge, then told to rendezvous at the infamous cupboard. As if scripted, Mr. Travis asked his favorite question, and to his surprise and delight I choose the largest cane within his arsenal, for I was determined not to show any signs of fear. The rest of the class looked on with curious anticipation as I lifted my head on high and turned it away from Travis as if to ignore the event and the impending pain. He firmly held my hand in place ready to strike it with a vigor that would not be fulfilled, for as he began to deliver the blow the cane disintegrated to a fine powder, which fell softly to the floor like a gentle snowfall. Although the class was confused at this site, a lone teetering chuckle could be heard, which soon came to a halt with the angry Mr. Travis who had now turned to find more victims. I could see he was also baffled, yet more than that, he appeared to look simply cheated of his game, mumbling, "Must have been woodworm or some such thing." His determination was steadfast, and once more the cupboard was opened. Again I was asked to choose another instrument to resolve his need, but the open cupboard displayed the same large cane that I had previously selected. All eyes stared in disbelief then immediately darted to the floor where those powdered remnants had fallen, but alas, there were no signs of them ever being there. At this point Mr. Travis nervously excused me with eyes full of suspicion, and never again was I asked to journey to that fateful cupboard.

Even to this day I have never understood the purpose of inflicting pain in connection to the learning process, but I believe it was of more benefit to the one dispensing rather than the one receiving.

At the age of twelve this kind of domination culminated one day. Our homeroom teacher Mr. Alritage, an older man of sour disposition, was easily identified by his long, flowing, black cloak, which often reminded me of a vampire in transition. With it he always wore a red accessory beneath, be it vest or tie. We nicknamed him Red Al. On one occasion Mr. Alritage invited me to the blackboard to complete a divisional sum, which he had carefully arranged. On my arrival the chalk was handed to me, along with a smug glance from him. I stood facing the mathematical equation unable to comprehend it for what seemed an eternity, while suffering the occasional sarcasms given with an obvious relish. Mathematics had always been my weakest subject, and on that particular day, Mr. Alritage was determined to make an example of me, though for what purpose I will never know. The final disgrace came when he silently approached me from behind clasping the back of my head in his broad hand. He then proceeded to direct my head from side to side in order to erase the sum from the blackboard with my nose, indicating that my head did have a use after all. The rest of the class thought this sight was hilarious and enjoyed the entertainment value thoroughly. Shortly after, as I turned to face the class and my tormentor, they noticed with surprise that there were no chalk marks on my nose, yet the sum on the board had been erased. How could this be without chalk residue? Then, strangely, all was revealed for as Mr. Alritage turned, his nose and cheeks showed those missing chalk marks. Suddenly aware of his dilemma, Alritage began vigorously rubbing his red face, which now matched his red vest. He vented his anger toward the giggling class with a three-day detention that quickly changed their mood.

I knew there were forces at work here seemingly protecting me from harm, which all were completely beyond my control or understanding. Consequently there were many, especially Mr. Alritage and Mr. Travis, who now treated me with distain combined with an obvious suspicion, and they would often simply ignore my presence. I also noticed that Teddy no longer worked his bully tactics on me. Had I gained a reputation of sorts? If so, it certainly worked to my benefit, and yet there was an uncomfortable feeling of suspicion and doubt. The lack of wisdom and the basic understanding of what can truly motivate children from these elders left me with a confused and untutored gap, which I eventually realized was the exception rather than the rule. It was firmly well established during early childhood that my scholastic abilities in the world of academia would be somewhat lacking; yet my artistic and creative abilities surged on, and painting the natural beauty of my surroundings would grow to become my forte and passion in life.

Mam was not aware of all these events, besides she was too busy working to maintain our survival. Triumphantly she escaped the cotton mills and obtained work in a car sales garage as a valet, cleaning and polishing vehicles of all shape and size. The work was a little easier as she wasn't playing catch-up to a non-stop, merciless cotton machine. At night she worked in a theater or the "flix" as we called it, as an usher, occasionally allowing me entry to see a free film. During those early years, it seemed that Mam worked a great deal of the time while I was often left to my own devices. I suspect this scenario somewhat cast the mold of who I am today: comfortable as a quiet introvert but unpredictable with the occasional glimpse of the extrovert when I found it to be necessary.

It was around this time that I had noticed some small changes to my birthmark. It had grown both in size and color, especially in the tree's foliage for it now appeared a dark shade of green. But I thought little of it at the time and simply put it down to the growing years.

Mam and I had moved around from place to place, but they all looked much the same to me. Then the owner of the garage where Mam worked offered us a three room flat, which he also owned. It had a living room, bedroom, and kitchen, which contained a high bath that had an attached wooden lid. When closed, we could use it as a kitchen table, which I thought was quite unique. We were a step up in the world — not a big step, but nonetheless we were moving forward.

I soon became friends with some of the local lads, and Peter Foster became my closest pal. A bond of friendship instantly emerged between us that went beyond mere words, and although I was often nominated "peculiar" by many, Peter, a quiet, easy-to-please lad, accepted my so-called peculiarities without question. He towered above all other boys his age, thus he was labeled "big Peter." On occasion he would be made to care for his younger brother, David. Of course, we all took a shared responsibility of also caring for him, but naturally playing would always be our priority for the day. Young David was easy to recognize by the permanent candle that occupied the base of his nose running down (forgive the pun) to his upper lip. Among our fraternity, handkerchiefs were in short supply, and well, "a girl thing." Speaking of which, the girls were not impressed by David's constant accessory, but it never really bothered me until one day when we had a scuffle, and a portion of the candle became dislodged and was now located on me. Our friendship remained steadfast, but I was now more aware of that vertical beacon and my proximity to it.

My pocket money allowance was limited, just enough for a weekly sweetie (candy) need, which consisted in total of one Cowan's toffee bar; however, if I had two pennies more, I could get a chocolate-coated version. This, of course, was a bonus. I would proceed to break the bar into several pieces, so if I ate one piece a day, it could last all week.

On occasion, in order to add to my limited allowance, I would gather old clothes from the neighborhood and sell them to the local "rag man" who was easily recognized, for he would often wear those flea-infested garments, changing his attire when the mood required it. We nicknamed him "Itch," because of the obvious. Itch would pay a miserly rate determined by the weight of your goods. In order to balance the scales to my advantage, I would daringly add stones or an occasional small, metal bar to pockets that had zips or buttons on them. Of course, it didn't take long to be discovered, and consequently I was banned from the "rag man's" door. There ended my life of crime.

From an early age I recall Saturday afternoons at the matinees was a must with a theater full of children constantly moving and shouting. Then a film that completely captured my thirst for adventure where good would always triumph over evil was *Robin Hood* with Errol Flynn, Olivia De Haveland, and Basil Rathbone. It was a lighthearted, American version of a local hero who many believed to be fictitious. Certainly the film's humorous theme would add to that belief.

Peter and I went from the cowboy gun battles to Robin and his merry band of thieves. We made bows from bamboo shoots and obtained arrows from off-cuts at the local lumberyard. A nail would be attached at one end by cutting notches with a thin wire wrapping the nail to the notched shaft of the arrow. The opposing end was spliced to insert thin handmade cardboard feathers. They worked really well until one fateful day when I accidentally shot an arrow into Peter's foot. With some medical care he was okay, but our bow and arrows were forever banned. My guilt lasted for many weeks thereafter; at least until my friend was up and about again, but, of course, Peter's mam would continue to remind me just in case I should forget.

Our Secret Site

I was now sixteen years old, and time had raced to 1957. This would be an amazing year of revelation and discovery for both my friend and me. Luck had descended upon me, for Mam now acquired something I had always dreamed of but could never afford. A bicycle, second hand of course — but that didn't matter. Naturally, I couldn't wait to put hundreds of miles on it.

With the start of the summer holidays, which for me was a time of pure joy and freedom, Peter and I decided a journey of discovery into the lush countryside of Yorkshire would be on our agenda. Peter was also a bike enthusiast, so in turn we decided to make a day of it on our two wheel steeds. I recall that day as one that time would never let us forget. With sandwiches clumsily crammed into pockets, we departed. While in the country, we aimlessly traveled hill and dale with the wind at our backs and the warm rays of the sun on our faces. How could life be better than this? Eventually we entered a quiet, wooded area sign-posted private property, but surely it couldn't be meant for us. Anyway, we parked our bikes in a nearby gully ready to proceeded on foot. Imaginations began to soar as our trek wound its way through the lush forest for some two miles. We finally reached the base of a steep hill and climbed it. This finally brought us to an open field, which we crossed to the continuing forest. Shortly thereafter in a remote dense area of unbroken overgrowth and by total accident, we stumbled upon something so very unexpected, almost as if trying to hide. There it was. A large, leaning grave stone surrounded by the remnants of an old, iron, picket fence. A short distance away there was a huge, old oak tree and surrounding its girth, a wooden seat in urgent need of repair but perhaps beyond it. We slowly approached this very old-looking head stone that was heavily moss ridden. With eyes getting larger by the second, we began to read in old English text, "Hear lies Robert, Earl of Huntingdon, He was the peoples' champion called Robin Hood." There were other inscribed words, but they were not legible partly due to the heavy moss along with many cracks to broken portions of the stone, which had firmly taken possession of it. The site appeared to be untouched and unattended for a very long time. I considered that what we were witnessing very few others had. Peter and I stood frozen at the site, and for a moment we dared not breath. Unable to move we stood confused yet mesmerized as our imaginations ran amuck. I was unsure of this man's true existence according to fable or fact, and certainly that film entertainment now seemed a distant memory. For what we had just witnessed was indeed real and I knew this site held many wondrous secrets. We soon realized that the day's clock was running away from us, and it was time to return home. I believe a little fear of the unknown also helped to prompt our departure. We swore not to tell anyone. It would be our secret, but I was haunted by the day's events, and although Peter and I spoke little of that day, I knew there was unfinished business about the whole thing. Even as we considered returning to again find that intriguing site, a hesitation persisted.

Two weeks later we both realized that in spite of our fears, we had to satisfy our hungry curiosity. There was simply no choice but to revisit the grave site that must have held intriguing secrets. It was mid July when on a sunny start to the day, Peter and I once more departed. Two hours later we again reached the wooded beginning to our journey on foot. The private-property sign was gone, but it didn't matter for we were indifferent to it anyway. We noticed some subtle changes to the foot trail, which did not seem as obvious as before. Finally, we reached the base of that hill, and our pace became slower partly because of the journey but also with some anticipation of what could be ahead. It was a good excuse to stop and take a rest, so at this point from our jacket pockets, we retrieved crushed sandwiches wrapped in paper and shared our one bottle of ginger pop. I still had two pieces of toffee left, a piece for each of us, and that became our dessert. We were now fed, rested, and ready to continue our journey. Again we climbed that hill to the open field, which was now ablaze with a sea of giant daisies, all dancing to the whim of the wind but intermittently basking in the rays of the sun when permitted. I thought how quickly they had grown. Peter and I crossed the field picking some of the flowered gems on route, so that we could place them at the grave site. Once again we entered the forest getting nearer to our destination and found ourselves without realizing it, walking just a little closer to each other. Ahead was the site, but the shrub and bush growth appeared to be less than before. Slowly advancing toward the grave site and to our surprise, we noticed some differences from our original discovery. For example, the headstone was now standing almost upright, and the inscribed words on the stone were now more legible. The grass in the area was shorter and greener. Even the iron picket fence surrounding the grave appeared to stand more erectly. Not a word was uttered as our searching eyes now shifted toward that ancient, giant oak tree. We noticed that the man-made seat surrounding it still required some repair and yet less than before. It seemed obvious that someone must have been here, trying to repair and upkeep the years of damage that time had imposed on this place. We decided to sit on a portion of the unbroken seat in order to absorb all that surrounded us. While there, I noticed a hand cut and very well worn inscription, which we had obviously missed on our first hurried visit. It read: "Neath this tree lies the true heart of England," Just below those words, I discovered what looked like an arrow head embedded in its bark. I tried to extract and retrieve the ancient prize but was unable to even move it. We placed our daisy gatherings in a notched hole located on the seat directly below those inscribed words. The day's light was slowly beginning to fade. Twilight now provided that sense of intrigue, and with it, we became a little overwhelmed again with the unknown just waiting to expose itself. Reluctantly, we decided to leave our secret site, and yet there must be at least another who had been there to upkeep it, but who?

On my return home Mam asked, "Where have you been today? You're late again!" I informed her that Peter and I had journeyed far and discovered Robin Hood's grave, and today we had made a return visit. Then I realized I had just broken our secret, but as I predicted, without slowing the rhythm of her housework, Mam smiled and replied, "That's nice, dear, but I hope you are not playing with those dreadful bow and arrows." I reassured her that we were not.

As I sat contemplating all that had happened, my dreams of a wondrous world just waiting to be discovered now began to stir and perhaps become a reality. My mind often struggled to be liberated from the small and boring realities imposed by the will of captive spirits who were resigned to their fate and given the chance others. I now felt an enchanting adventure was about to begin.

Our secret site -- Robin's grave.

A JOURNEY OF DESTINY

Three more days had passed and Peter and I felt it was again time for a visit to our secret site. Yes, it still must have been a secret as Mam obviously thought that I was fantasizing when she had asked our whereabouts that day. This time we were well equipped for any eventuality. I found Dad's old army satchel in which we packed a box of matches, a flashlight, a small scout's knife, a blanket, a packed lunch for two, my grandfather's watch, a pad of paper and pencil along with an old box brownie camera. We knew no one would believe our story, so it would be necessary to take pictures of the site — yet did we really want others to know of our discovery? Off we went now well equipped. Once again, we mounted our trusty bikes, and with eager anticipation, peddled our way to the site. As before, we parked our bicycles and traveled on foot through the forest, but now noticed that the path had further changed. It was more overgrown, and at times not easy to find. After a few moments of head scratching and puzzlement, we decided to continue. Again the forest looked different with what seemed to be now a lighter growth, but the day was overcast and heavy with cloud, so we simply put it down to the light of day playing it's tricks. We also noticed that the temperature had dropped considerably for we could now see each other's breath. There were so many changes. Something was not right. Climbing the hill we eventually reached the open field where to Peter's and my surprise there was a light sprinkling of snow. How could this be? It was the height of summer. What was happening and why? Peter's eyes now showed a genuine reluctance to go on, and so I suggested that he wait and keep a vigil at this place, but for me, in spite of the fear, there seemed to be little choice. I was compelled to know more, and so I became locked into what was about to unfold. My friend pleaded for me not to continue, but I was stubbornly adamant. He finally offered to wait 30 minutes for my return, after which if I did not show, he would go to the nearest village for help. I was now alone, and with satchel in hand, I slowly proceeded across the hard ground of the field before me. Once more within the forest I could see the site ahead, but it appeared to be more exposed than before. Upon entering it, and again to my surprise, I noticed many differences from our last inspection. Now the gravestone was standing perfectly erect, and it was smooth and clean of moss and weather damage. All the inscribed words were easy to read, but something was missing; the iron picket fence was no longer there. My eyes now jumped to the old oak tree, which somehow looked more youthful than before. I noticed that the carved words on its bark appeared to be freshly cut. As I sat on the tree's surrounding bench, which now had no signs of damage, I noticed there were still remnants of wood slivers that appeared to have fallen from the above carving onto the seated portion, below.

I sat and pondered all that surrounded me, yet nothing seemed to make any sense. There and then I decided to retrieve the box brownie camera from my satchel, so I could visually record what was before me. I positioned the camera toward the gravestone, and in peering through the viewfinder, I discovered there was no grave in its site, only brush and grass. Were my eyes playing tricks? Then I focused on the tree with its inscribed words. Although the tree was there, the bench and those words were not. It strangely seemed that the eye of the camera could not see what my own eyes could. I nervously placed the camera back into the satchel, and as I did, the silence of the forest was broken by a distant haunting noise of what sounded like a sheep's horn. The noise startled me, and with it, I dropped the satchel. Now considering my retreat, I slowly backed away from the site with eyes searching every part of my surroundings. As my fears increased so did my pace. Moments later, I could see Peter in the distance but when approaching, I realized that I had forgotten the satchel. Only yards away from my friend, I signaled my dilemma and now my intent to go back to retrieve our goods. Peter, now frozen to his spot with fear, had also heard that haunting sound and yelled, "No, please don't go back! It doesn't matter!" But I was headstrong and determined. This time I decided to run and did so stirring the occasional bird and rabbit. Quickly reaching the site, to my astonishment, there was nothing there but the old oak tree. The grave site was not there, and the tree's inscription and seat were also missing, along with my satchel. What was going on? All reason had left as I stood there allowing my breath and my senses to be regained. Then once again I heard the sound of that horn, this time much closer and now accompanied by human voices. My heart began to pound, and from the corner of one eye I turned to see a large stag bounding in the opposite direction of the commotion, and so I decided to follow his lead. After some hard running, I now realized that Peter must be only steps away, but *wait*, the field was no longer there, and my friend was not in site. I called his name, but there was no response. Had I taken a wrong turn? Me, impossible! The terrain looked similar, yet there was a thicker coat of green all around. Everything seemed to be changing from moment to moment. I was now all alone and felt unsure of what lay ahead. It was as if I had entered into another world, and to make things worse daylight seemed to be falling faster than it normally should. For a brief moment I thought of Mam's anger at my tardy return home which strangely sounded good at this point.

Fears of the unknown once more began to grow as a repeat of that haunting horn was again sounded, and I now heard the voices of men closing in on my location. Unsure of where to go I decided to hide in the heavy growth of the woods. The sound of horses galloping furiously drew closer, as the ground beneath me began to tremble. Then as I nervously peered through the bushes, there they were — around a dozen men, seeking who or what, I don't know. Strangely, they were dressed in what looked like Norman medieval soldiers uniforms and led by an angry, evil-looking fellow riding a large, snorting, black horse. His attire was also black with a hooded cloak that covered himself and most of the beast he was riding, giving the appearance of man and horse being as one. As they passed and rode into the distance, I sat confused and puzzled by all these strange events but soon came to realize there was little I could do until the light of day returned. I reluctantly decided to bed down for the evening as dusk had now quickly thickened into darkness. I found a gully with an overhang that would both hide and protect me from the elements. My senses were acute and I slept little listening to the sounds of the night, which included an owl and something that sounded larger as it foraged through the woodland. Also during the night the rain came and washed everything clean including the heaviness of dread from the air. The revitalized shrubs and small trees had grown a heavy coat of green, which appeared to surround and protect me from the elements of the night. But my mind lingered, and it could not forget the many things that just did not make sense. Trying to rationalize them simply added to my state of bewilderment.

THE SANCTUARY

The early morning slowly awoke with a growing light that began to stretch and penetrate its beams through the forest. The enchanting seduction before me gave a fresh, breathtaking beauty that inspired me to explore its depths. I now felt completely safe and at one with my surroundings, and yet reality nagged and would not allow me to forget the puzzling events of yesterday. Where was I? And where was Peter? I knew he was fearful of what had happened, but I also knew my friend would not willingly desert me.

It was time to find some answers, and so I stepped a few paces to the stream below in order to refresh and wash myself. The waters were cold, clear, and clean. I noticed my reflection showed that birthmark, which had once more changed. It was again larger and the tree's foliage had now become a brighter green. Questions were in dire need of answers, and so I proceeded on foot still unsure of my direction. I knew the sun rose in the east, and so I decided to travel northeast in what I thought was our point of entry into the forest. My journey through the lush greenery of these woods was somehow familiar and yet not from recent travels. The comfort of these surroundings provided a reassurance that I had never known before.

After traveling for almost an hour I noticed something in the distance that appeared familiar to me. On closer arrival I saw that same oak tree where it all began and quickly realized that I had walked in a large circle. At that moment I thought, *how odd for me with my keen ability for direction.* It was as if the forest, and all things within it, were suggesting and willing the very path on which to walk.

I decided to climb a smaller tree close by. Perhaps I could get a better idea of which way to proceed. In doing so, I noticed not far away what looked like smoke, which could mean people. With new anticipation I traveled toward the smoke through what I thought was the heaviest growth I had seen in the forest. As I slowly got closer, an unusual and eerie silence descended. Climbing a small hill, I saw before me a site that took me by surprise. There I observed smoke and gases billowing from within a great hole in the ground. Cautiously approaching and on closer inspection I noticed giant, thorny, bramble bushes stretched some twenty-feet wide and ten-feet high surrounding and seemingly protecting the giant hole from entry.

Then after a few moments, a small tree before my very eyes began to grow up and over that thorny bush, while spreading its sprawling and leaning branches toward the protected, gaping hole. It was as if the tree now provided a means of entry, and a path along its branches now became obvious on which to walk.

The sites that lay before me continued to amaze and baffle, and although there was caution, I was surprised by the fact that I had no real fear of it all. As I stood there pondering the scene, there was a distinct feeling that I was being watched. Moments later I slowly inched closer to the tree as if drawn by an invisible force, and I soon found myself climbing upon it carefully stepping my way toward that strange but inviting hole, which must have been at least seventy-feet wide. The branch that I stood on gently and slowly leaned itself closer to the edge of that large crevice, and peering into its endless fiery depths, I noticed a giant, stone, spiraling staircase built into the walls of it, which plummeted to uncertain depths below. Now moving off the tree's branch to the edge of this circular tomb, the mighty tree began to retract itself, quickly disappearing back from where it came. Now there was, of course, no choice but to move down the staircase, and in doing so, I noticed dozens of tunnels feeding from it at intervals of about every ten yards. As it was my sixteenth year, I decided to pick tunnel number sixteen for entry. Slowly I descended the giant staircase. While passing each tunnel, I noticed their entrance provided a seductive whistling wind that enticed my entry. But steadfastly I carefully counted each opening finally reaching the chosen one, which unlike the others was calm and quiet. Slowly I entered into its dark and unknown recesses, unaware of what would lay before me. My steps took me upwards, sometimes walking but mostly climbing further into this unknown chasm. *But wait!* Ahead I could see the tunnels end with a glowing bright blue light coming from a source below and beyond. Reaching its glow now before me and to my utter amazement lay the most beautiful sight I had ever beheld. There was a grotto of immense size, and yet a grotto like no other I had ever seen. The wonders of this underground garden contained two waterfalls one above the other. Each created its own pool below. Lastly these waters all rested in a crystal clear lagoon, which I later discovered were fed by underground thermal waters, surrounded by trees and plants of all kind and size. The brilliant light and air within seemed to find their source from those magical waters. At the tunnel's edge I found myself standing some 70 feet above the lagoon, and quickly realized that there was no safe way in which to enter this world when once more a tree below offered its service and began to extend its branches to my waiting feet. This repeated phenomenon was completely beyond my comprehension, yet I was drawn to oblige it. As before, I stepped onto and moved down the tree's branch descending to the ground below, and as I stood there uncertain of which way to proceed, I felt those eyes once more upon me.

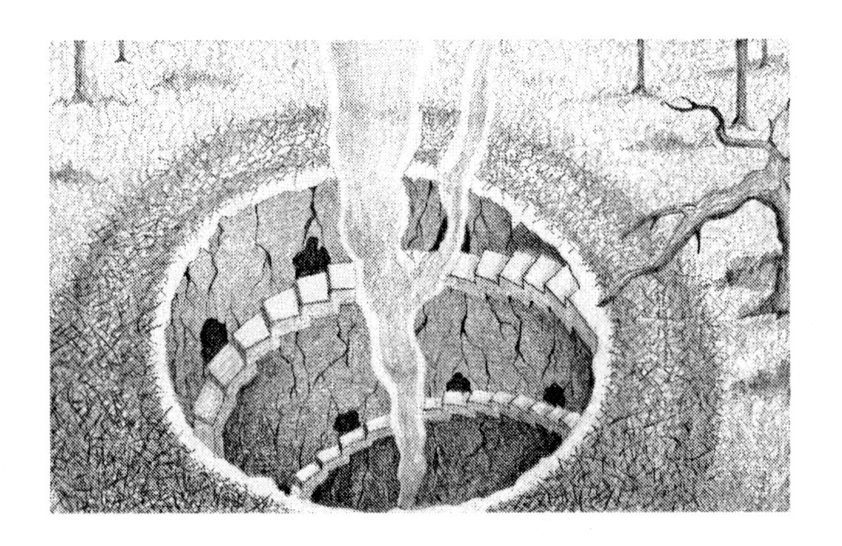

Entry to the santuary

The Meeting

The garden's beauty embraced me as I peered into it and scanned my surroundings. Suddenly without warning it all started to move and in various directions. I rubbed my eyes in disbelief, but the movement continued now mainly towards me. Whatever they were, I now noticed that they had two legs of a sort and the vague appearance of human form, yet they were well disguised. I could now see these creatures numbering about 50 were armed with spears, knives, and bows and arrows. *But wait!* As they drew closer I began to realize that they were all young people, mostly adolescent boys and girls around my age clothed in tunics that appeared to be made from tree foliage, which allowed that excellent camouflage. Then one of the taller boys removed his leafy hood to expose a youthful face framed by a mop of long, black hair. He calmly asked, "What is thy name, and where doest thou come from?" *What a strange way to ask a question,* I thought, and as I was about to reply, one of the girls who I would guess to be around 15 abruptly shouted, "Look! He bears the sign." Now all eyes were riveted upon my open shirt and exposed chest. Moments later they all fell to their knees chanting, "Woodargon, Woodargon..." Confused, and a little annoyed, I firmly asked them to stop. Looking directly at the taller boy who I presumed to be their leader, I replied, "My name is Robert Wilson, and I am from the town of Uddersfeld."

Then the taller lad asked, "What year is this?" and with curiosity I replied, "Well, 1957, of course." I went on to explain all the events that led to this moment, and although their silence was almost deafening, they appeared to show little surprise of my tale. In fact there were some reassuring smiles from my words. I remarked that, "Those watchful eyes were upon me long before I had entered this world."

"Why wait until this moment?" one of the smaller boys exclaimed. "Those were not the eyes of the tree people you see before you. You were being observed by Pook. Pook is the local faerie also known as the Poogoblin of our woods. He can be a troublemaker, but he is usually quite harmless. That is, unless he takes a dislike to you, but he knows that to harm a friend of the forest is to bring harm unto himself. Pook's mischievous ways can be most annoying, and on several occasions he has been banned from the sanctuary. Yet he continues to return, usually because he is bored or lonely, and he will often beg for someone to play with him. The tree world puts up with his mischievous ways although I am unsure why."

I had many questions but my main concern was for news of Peter. I impatiently asked, "What of my friend, Peter. He is a larger boy dressed like me."

"He lives," said one. "We have him safe in the inner sanctuary, and he is at present with John Little."

"He was lucky not to have been taken by the Black Death," said another. I was now silently beside myself with joy, ignoring just exactly what the Black Death was.

Now becoming more and more impatient, I asked, "Who are you people, and where am I?"

Their leader finally responded. "Our time is 1247 in the year of our Lord, and your coming was foretold long before your time. Our guardian's days are coming to an end." He went on to explain that their guardian was the Earl of Huntingdon, also known among the people as Robin Hood, for he is almost the last of his kind.

Incredibly I began to realize that time had somehow pulled us back to another place, but still the whys and hows continued to dance frantically in my head. In a state of confused disbelief, I asked, "But what of the elders, the parents and grandparents of these children?"

With heads bowed the slow response came. "They were members of Robin's band, and all were betrayed and killed; even their wives who lived in the village suffered that same fate. Robin and John Little were the only ones to escape, and it was they who saved us and taught us how to survive in this world."

Still confused, I tried to recall the tale of when King Richard returned from the Crusades. Surely truth and fairness once more returned to England, but as their leader explained, those good years lasted but a few. Then Richard became ill and bedridden with the sleeping sickness, which came from his many years on the Crusades. His formerly banished younger brother, John, again returned and forced his way to power.

Frustrated, I asked, "Would someone please bring my friend Peter to me?"

Then a young lad emerged, nodded his head in acknowledgement, and said, "Your man will be here forthwith." I asked the leader his name and he exclaimed with pride, "I am called 'the Scarlet'. My father was known as Will Scarlet."

When I asked of his father, the Scarlet sadly replied, "Like many in our band he was betrayed and slain by the evil Bishop of this shire who we thought to be a friend of the people, but his greed for power and money exceeded even that of the Sheriff's.

A trap had been set for all in the band and only Robin and John escaped. But Robin suffered injury and within a year his sight was gone. This, though, was enough time to organize our survival in this world you see before you. Robin has lived in these Woods for some three score years and became at one with our friends, the trees. Our home, the 'sanctuary,' is a gift from the tree world above, but our days in this world will soon be at an end, for it has been foretold that our sanctuary will be thrust to the world of our ancestors above. You have been chosen to lead us back to our ancestral home in that world."

I stared in disbelief at his words and considered that surely a mistake must have been made. Why and how could Peter and I become involved in such a bazaar tale? The Scarlet replied, "All will be revealed when you meet with the Woodargon."

I could now see my friend Peter accompanied by a large man with a limp emerging from behind the upper waterfall. They descended to the ground below by means of a path that seesawed its way to where we were standing. With sighs of relief, Peter and I hugged. The larger man introduced himself as John Little and said, "We have been awaiting your coming." I judged John to be a robust man of some 60 or more years, proudly standing about six feet six inches tall. When I asked how he had become injured, he replied, "When Robin and I were young lads before our skills of weaponry were acquired, we played a foolish game with bow and arrow, and I was accidentally shot in the foot. The injury healed well, but some years later I began to develop the limp you now see."

I immediately turned a sympathetic eye to my friend Peter and whispered, "Sorry." Peter simply blinked and smiled in return, and then I asked my friend, "What happened to you."

He replied, "When I saw you returning to retrieve the satchel, the field before me began to disappear and woodland rapidly grew upon it. Confused, I decided to wait for your return, which I thought would only be a minute or two. Then I heard them — men on horseback galloping with frenzy, and they were almost upon me when without warning and to my surprise leafy tree vines quickly descended and gathered around me to hold my being. I was hurled upwards into the trees as the horsemen rode by. There, I rested on a branch, and suddenly the tree became alive with movement, for all about me were these tree people.

The Scarlet, who I would guess to be around 18 years old, exclaimed, "Here is your bag. We took it from 'Pook' who often likes to take things without asking. Because of its size and weight, he didn't get far. His crimes are usually punishable by the trees that constantly watch and reprimand him with a sound spanking from a willowy branch or two." The Scarlet now with purpose in his voice said, "It is time for both guardians to meet, for there is much to be said."

So Peter, the tree people, and I followed the Scarlet up a path a short distance to the first waterfall at the base of the grotto. We soon found ourselves entering another cave-like tunnel located behind the falling waters and walked some 20 yards to a smaller grotto filled with ground-level lime stalagmites. Moving forward, we zigzagged our way through the giant needles until reaching an open area, which contained many ceiling stalactites. The middle of this arena contained a small plateau where I could now see a man reclining on a bed of soft, flaxen leafs. I presumed it was Robin, He was a handsome man of around 60 looking every part the regal leader that he was, as he proudly turned to anticipate our arrival. I soon realized that this man was blind, for no eye contact was made, but his reassuring smile eased our uncertainty. In a deep and mature voice, he said, "Welcome Robert and Peter to the 'sanctuary.' We have long awaited your coming."

Almost in disbelief I asked, "Are you the famous Robin Hood?"

He smiled and said, "Some would say infamous, but yes, I am he."

I continued, "What is the meaning of this word, 'Woodargon?' Robin explained that the name means "lord and keeper of the woods above and this sanctuary below." He then proceeded to open his tunic to expose that familiar birthmark of the tree, which was identical to mine. In turn I inadvertently showed my own, and immediately there appeared a bright, blue beam of light coming from this great man's birthmark. To my surprise it slowly came toward me and entered mine. On its contact the cave lit up with an intense brightness that forced all eyes to be covered — all but Robin's, of course. The beam finally withdrew itself from Robin and was now retracting itself into me.

Now looking weak and tired, Robin beckoned me to stand beside him and as I did he rested his hand on my shoulder saying, "My time is coming to an end, and you have been chosen to be the new guardian of the tree people. Soon, you will lead them to a safe world in the home of our ancestors above."

Still confused I asked, "But why me?"

Robin explained, "Your blood is that of my sister, Margola, who against my father's wishes fell in love and married the first keeper of this forest who was a woodsman called Lorben. Margola left the house of Locksley and eloped with Lorben to the world you now see before you. The woodsman would not join our band of outcasts for he was a man of peace and tranquility. Although he was not a participant, over the years he did come to support our cause. Together, with the permission of the tree world, we were allowed to live here in the sanctuary. Lorben was the first 'Woodargon' of this world. Then on his passing, I, with his blessing, became the next 'Woodargon.' You will be the last and final 'Woodargon' chosen to do battle with the evil ones of this land and to bring a lasting peace to the world of our ancestors.

"We seek only peace and justice, but the Bishop of this shire who is also known as Vargis, has, in the name of evil, pillaged, sacked, and killed, so that his coffers remain full. He pays and uses the services of the Sheriff who is called 'the black death.' These Norman demons will stop at nothing to have their gain. Knowing full well of this, and fearful for the future of our land, King Richard secretly had the crown of England sent to my trust, and asked that it be placed above the eye of the great needle, which is embedded atop the rock called the 'pinnacle.' It is said that from this place only the true heir of this realm will have the power to remove it and rid this land of evil once and for all. You, Robert, have come to us from a world beyond our time to fulfill your destiny.

"Not long after the traitorous attack on our band, my sister Margola came to me with a prophecy that just before my death, there would be a third and final 'Woodargon' come from a time far beyond our own. It was foretold that our bloodline would produce only females for eight hundred years, but the prophecy requires a male child born with the sign of the tree. You, Robert, are that male child. But enough for now, I tire of the day and there will be much to speak of on the morrow."

With those words a maiden of great beauty came forward, took my hand and that of Peter's and escorted us to an inner chamber where there was food and beds of flax. The lass was about to retreat when I asked her name and if she would stay awhile and join us in our meal. She responded, "As you wish, my Lord, but only for a short while. My name is Roxelena, and I am unsure who my parents were for they died when I was a babe, but I believe they came from the village of Uddersfeld in the world above. Yet it is strange that no one in our band can say for sure." She turned her head away as tears began to well in the corners of her eyes while she tried to hide them with a wall of long, golden hair that now came between us. Then intent on a hasty retreat, she said, "Is there anything else you would wish for, my Lord."

I tried to console her and asked that she sit beside me and continue. "I seek but a few answers about the world above. There must surely be good people that live in the village of Uddersfeld and what of their plight?" Roxelena described their hardships living under the rule of such evil men. She went on, "These people exist through the grace of their faith, but they have no place in which to worship as the Bishop has banned entry to all holy places. Anyone found disobeying his rule will suffer instant death, and so they offer prayer in the safety and privacy of their own dwellings. The Bishop along with the Sheriff are in league with the devil, and they with their followers have great power over the will of good men. You have seen 'the black death' when you first entered the world above. He knows of our existence, and patrols our woodland daily in hopes of finding and killing us." In closing, Roxelena said, "I must take my leave for you should rest before the day of revelations." And with that she was gone.

I immediately felt that Roxelena was indeed a special person in both character and beauty, for a glow seemed to surround and follow her with warmth that gave a reassuring comfort. And so, with that fond thought we were bedded, and soon thereafter entered the land of slumber.

Robin's destiny fulfilled

Peter and I awoke the following morning to find a tray of bread, milk, and fruit sitting beside us. Peter exclaimed, "I wasn't sure if this was all a dream, but I now see that it is not." He continued, "I have discovered that John Little is an ancestor and distant relative going back some eight hundred years, yet how can this be?"

I replied, "I, too, have asked this very question but have come to realize that on occasion the fate of man lies outside his control. Both you and I must walk this path of uncertainty to its end."

Roxelena now quietly entered our abode and asked that we attend the guardian with haste for his time is closing, and there was much to be revealed. So my friend and I followed the maiden to again meet with Robin. As we entered his chamber we noticed that all the tree people were somberly gathered surrounding his bedded plateau. Robin now appeared sitting on the edge of his bed looking much weaker and very tired. He beckoned me forward to a large chest sitting beside him. Slowly reaching into it, he retrieved a plain wooden cross. Putting the cross around my neck, he said, "This cross was a gift from my only beloved, Marian, who, because of all the violence and evil of our time, decided to join a nunnery." He continued with heavy heart to explain that some years later, the coughing sickness came upon her. "Before her untimely passing, she gave me the cross saying wear the sign of Christ when in the presence of evil. It will serve you well." With hesitation he then reached to the ground and beside the chest, he lifted a finely carved, wooden staff some seven feet long. "This was also a gift, from Lorben, our first 'Woodargon.' From his love of nature came this staff. It has great powers, for it will do the bidding of your thoughts, but it will not take life."

Robin turned to face me as his eyes met my own, and for a moment I believe he could actually see me. With authority he said, "You are now the 'Woodargon' of the sanctuary and the tree world above. Along with this title, you must obey the laws of nature and protect all living things within this land. You have been chosen to lead the tree people to a safe world above, for the sanctuary will soon be raised unto that world. You must rid this land of the evil that reins and bear allegiance to the true heir of this realm." Robin then called for Roxelena to come forward. She approached with head bowed as Robin exclaimed, "You never knew of your parents, child, for I was sworn to secrecy, but now is the time of revelations, for I have fulfilled my promise. You are Roxelena, daughter and only child to the royal family of Queen Elena and King Richard." Shock descended, and all present fell to their knees in awe of those words. "The royal family sent you as a babe, to my care, knowing full well of the struggles to come." Robin continued, "You are to succeed to power on your sixteenth birthday, which comes in five days time. For it is at this time that the great battle for this land will begin at the site of the 'pinnacle.'" For the last time he reached back into the chest and from it he took a peasant's dowdy and torn hooded cape. With it, he wrapped and covered

Roxelena's shoulders. The cape appeared to swallow her up as it hung loosely and generously gathered at her feet. He then asked that she place her hand over her heart and on doing so the garment turned into a magnificent cape of red silk with three golden lions finely embroidered upon it. Robin declared, "This cape was given to me by King Richard — your father — and as you see, it bears his mark. It has the power to protect and hide the wearer from all manner of foe, but remember, you must cover your head with its hood when danger is present. Be not afraid and trust your hearts, for mine is with all of you. Your new 'Woodargon' will guide you to the world above. Give him your trust as you have with me. And now my time has come to an end for there are many that await me."

Now resigned to his fate, Robin slowly arose from his bed and with some uncertainty, stood erect as John Little reluctantly handed him his long bow along with one arrow. He looked to the ceiling above, and the stalactites began to retract creating a vertical tunnel to the world above, then Robin's last words were, "I send this arrow into the land of my ancestors, and where it will rest, so will my body." With all his remaining strength, he pulled the bow back and then released the arrow, which went straight and true into the world above. Robin then collapsed to his bed and took his last breath ending his life with a contented smile.

There was great sadness and sobbing among all present, for he was indeed a hero to these people. I looked toward John Little whose grief had become overwhelming, and I gently tugged on his sleeve quietly saying, "Come, John. You are Robin's oldest friend, and it is your quest to find the resting place of that arrow so that his will would be fulfilled."

John, my friend Peter, and I entered the world above. Not long after John cried, "Here! I have found the place." My friend and I quickly arrived to his location and sure enough there was the arrow firmly embedded in that mighty oak tree that Peter and I had come to know so well. John announced, "Beneath this tree will lie the true heart of England." And so it would be. There was a day of mourning and deep respect, for it was Robin and John Little who kept the children of the village of Uddersfeld alive and safe from the evils of the world above, and they had truly been taught well in the ways of survival. Our last farewell to Robin came on the following day as all were assembled at the site where it all began for Peter and me.

Surrounding his resting place a mist had slowly descended and with it came the shadowy figure of a maiden. John cried, "Look! It is the fair Marian." Her waiting was over. She had come to finally claim her Robin and with that, he arose from the earth, took the hand of his beloved, and walked off into the gray morning mist.

The gathering slowly dispersed, to be with their thoughts while I remained at the site that had become so familiar to me. The events that had just taken place now gave new meaning to them. I was unaware of Roxelena's presence as she slowly came toward me through that same mist and said, "I loved this man as a daughter would love a father, and I will miss him, for he has spent most of his life caring, nurturing, and protecting all that needed it. Now it is his time to rest in the valley of peace with his beloved Marian." Without realizing it, my hand easily fell into Roxelena's, and we stood there for the longest time without speaking. I recall thinking that our silence was saying far more than mere words could, and I felt a human comfort that I had not known before. We parted with an unspoken promise of a new tomorrow.

I returned to my chamber to find Peter deep in slumber, and so I, too, bedded down, but the events of the day lay heavy on my mind and sleep would not come easily. I arose and decided to relax with a swim in the lagoon. Entering the temperate and soothing waters, I soon discovered that there was another within the magic pool. Roxelena emerged from the clear depths below and exclaimed, "I, too, could not sleep." She then calmly asked, "May I wash you?" I later discovered that to offer the washing of a person was considered a mark of respect and had no physical attachment. But at that moment, my red face accompanied by a stammering *no* was my response, yet with some hesitation that surprised me.

"Anyway," I said, "remember you are of royal blood and your conduct should reflect that status." She smiled dismissively as she turned and swam toward the descending waters, then, disappeared into their cascades.

Observing the Foe

On the following day, a meeting was held in the garden chamber, which was aptly named for the surrounding beauty of its many plants and flowers. All assembled and sat around a giant mushroom. For a few moments there was an uncertain silence, then like a wave finding a beach, the sound of mutterings began to well and build. Roxelena was, of course, located at the head befitting her new status. Then a hush fell as the Scarlet rose to tell us of the festival of darkness, so named because the presence of evil was so strong that for three days, darkness would descend until the festival had concluded. He went on to say that once a year all the evil forces of this land would gather at the great pinnacle where many have attempted to remove and claim the royal crown of England but all have failed. "These futile attempts are now in their fifteenth year, but it is said that this year Vargis plans to use all the evil powers of this land and have them channeled through him so that collectively their powers along with his own will be more than enough for victory. Vargis hopes to walk the great needle's shaft, for he who succeeds will dislodge the crown and become the rightful heir to the throne of England. The festival of darkness and the walk of doom will take place on the same day as Roxelena's birthday and her right to royal ascension, so we must be prepared for the great battle ahead."

Many eager and impatient voices were in pursuit of doing battle yet with no plan for success, so I now stood to say, "We must be prepared for this great battle," and I asked that I be given two days in which to observe our foe and devise a plan. I requested that John, Peter, the Scarlet, and I go out into the village of Uddersfeld and on to the pinnacle to know more, so our plan would have purpose.

The Scarlet replied, "You are the 'Woodargon' and have complete authority within our ranks, so we will do as you ask."

Everyone nodded their agreement, then Roxelena stood and exclaimed in a determined voice. "I will join your group for if I am to be worthy of the crown, then I must also face the enemy. My father and Robin would expect no less."

The frown on my face gave way to a silent approval, but I added with my own determination, "Keep in mind, Roxelena, you must do as I ask." In turn she proudly nodded her agreement.

Shortly thereafter rumblings were both heard and felt within the sanctuary, which gave evidence that the area was becoming unsafe, for soon this world would be no more. It was decided that the tree people would leave the "sanctuary" on the second day of the "festival of darkness" and journey to meet us on the third day at the pinnacle, but they would remain within the safety of the forest which skirted the pinnacle by arrow distance and there await our instructions.

John Little stood and suggested that we visit the night sayer of soothes. He was the oldest and wisest man in the village. Sleeping during the light hours of day, he spent the evening hours gazing into the heavens above where many revelations have come to pass. The Bishop and Sheriff dismissed this man as a dreamer and a fool. In these times such men were left alone, for it was considered bad luck to bring harm to them.

The Scarlet informed us that the journey to the village would take the better part of a day, and the pinnacle was three leagues beyond. He also suggested that Peter and I would need a change of clothes for the journey. John also added that we should disguise and dress as peasants visiting the festival. We all agreed and now prepared for the journey ahead. A short time later we reassembled in the great hall chamber, looking as peasants of the day. I found the cloth to be rough against my skin, and my reluctance to wear tights was made clear when I desperately tried to hide those obvious areas, which Peter laughingly did not seem to be concerned about. As I gazed at Roxelena, I thought that even dressed in the shabbiest attire, she was still pleasant to the eye.

I soon found a connection to these people beginning to stir, and aside from the prophecy, I knew that Peter and I would commit to their plight no matter the outcome. Although not strong in number, we were truly strong in heart, and a well-devised plan could win the day. Now resigned to the quest ahead, we prepared to begin a journey that must be completed so that our destinies would be fulfilled. With enough food for three days, we said our farewells to the tree people and set forth into the world above. Our determination was now steadfast and on entering the forest, its density quickly swallowed us up. It was midday and we would not reach the village until mid evening. After some four hours of travel, we decided to sit and rest awhile. I noticed and chose a large stone for a seat, which provided a comforting warmth from the day's sun. Sliding over, I offered a portion of it to Roxelena, and then during our respite I again had that familiar feeling that we were being watched. A rustling sound from within the bushes could now be heard, so with hearty voice I asked the watcher to come forward and state their purpose. The Scarlet remarked, "Oh, it's only Pook."

A small but sturdy voice replied, "What do you mean, only Pook?" With that, out he jumped, standing no more than five inches from head to foot. Before me was an odd little fellow with clear wings and pointed ears that were typical of a Goblin. His devilish grin showed his two front teeth were missing. He said, "I know where you are going and of your plan. All I ask is that you and your band allow me to join your ranks. I can fight as good as any man here."

"Women of course don't count," Roxelena snarled at him.

He replied, "No offense was meant, fair Roxelena."

John exclaimed, "Why should we allow you to join our group, for you are no more than a troublemaker!"

Pook responded,

"I know that I have misbehaved in the past, and I admit the guilt, but in truth I am fearful of the evil ones who would rule this land harshly. Anyway, I can fly. Can any of you? I could be your eyes and ears and report all that I see."

I quickly considered his request and replied, "Indeed. why not? But any sign of trouble from you and you will be forever banned." Pook now appeared to be revitalized and excited at the prospects that lay ahead. I asked him to fly to the Bishop's castle and learn what he could of their plans. We would then meet again in the evening hours at the cottage of the sayer of soothes.

The Scarlet stood and said, "How do we know you won't betray us to the Bishop or the Sheriff?"

"You don't," said Pook, "but know this, that I would prefer to live in this world than that of the evil ones. After all, they just don't know how to have fun." And with a giggle, Pook darted off into the early night.

Curiosity began to stir and I turned to the Scarlet to ask of other goblins and why Pook was alone. The Scarlet informed me that recently the goblin world was forced to banish Pook for one year because of his many pranks. They considered him to be a throwback to a time when many goblins gained their reputation by the tricks and troubles they inflicted. Pook's punishment was to spend some time in the tree world and to learn the true values in that world. Scarlet, however, thought that the mold had been cast, for Pook was Pook, and Scarlet doubted he would ever change his mischievous ways.

Once again we departed for the cottage of the sayer of soothes, and again I felt a familiar kinship as my whole being surrendered to the hospitality and beauty of these woodlands. After two hours, we arrived at Boar's Crossroad where many creatures of the forest had gathered as if to greet us. A large and stately stag approached me, and I noticed a twinkle of knowledge from within those dark brown eyes. We knew that their world could be affected by the battle ahead, and although words were not exchanged, there was a silent understanding between us. Noticing the pace of our journey had slowed, I soon realized why. Two in our group were tiring and unable to keep up, so I asked all to gather to me and announced that the group should separate. Roxelena, John Little, and Peter would be traveling at the rear, while the Scarlet and I were to travel and scout ahead. We would all meet at the cottage. Roxelena with knitted brow gave that familiar questioning glance but was unable to argue the point.

Pook

Pook's Encounters

Pook had now reached the Bishop's castle, which displayed its menacing structure as the moon played hide and seek with the rolling clouds. Noticing a well-lit vertically slit window, he flew to the warmth of its light. Perched on an outer ledge, he could hear from within the menacing voices of the Bishop and the Sheriff. Deciding to get closer when all eyes had turned away, Pook darted to the enormous mantle above the fire, hiding in the shadows behind a large, ornamental, pewter chalice. He overheard the Bishop say to the Sheriff, "You must be sure that any threat to the success of our festival is stopped. I want patrols day and night for I know that those damn tree people will try to interfere in our quest."

The Sheriff nodded his agreement as he slowly backed a few paces to the mantle casually resting his arm upon it, only inches away from where Pook was hiding. With lightening speed he grabbed the heavy chalice behind which Pook was hiding and turning it upside down he brought it down and over Pook who now became a prisoner within the goblet's dome. The Bishop asked, "What are you doing, man?"

With a haughty laugh the Sheriff replied, "He didn't think I saw him for the goblin has truly been gobletted." The Sheriff looked at Pook with suspicion as one hand slowly released the cup's dome while his other hand blocked any escape. "It's that troublemaker – Pook."

The Bishop moved closer and asked, "What are you doing here?"

"Eh, well, I have come to join your mighty cause,"replied Pook.

The Bishop answered, "You have never joined our ranks before, so why now?"

Pook responded, "I'm tired of those boring tree people; they just don't know how to have fun. Anyway, you know of my reputation as a troublemaker, so why would I side with them?"

The Bishop moved closer and yelled, "Hold him upright." No sooner had the Sheriff done this than the Bishop grabbed both of Pook's wings and violently pulled them off. Pook screamed in pain, but in truth there was no pain for a goblin's wings fell off every month, and a new set replaced them within a few hours. As luck would have it, Pook was ready for a new set of wings anyway. The Sheriff and the Bishop were fully enjoying the agony that Pook was feigning, saying, "You will not be flying anywhere." Again putting the large goblet over Pook, Vargis snarled, "You will stay here until we decide what to do with you." Then both the Sheriff and the Bishop continued their evil plans unaware that Pook could hear them, because the Bishop had inadvertently trapped a portion of a small hair pin that was resting half in and half out of the chalice. Pook heard the pair scheming that all the soldiers would gather to surround and guard the pinnacle. Only those with the mark of evil would be allowed to pass. Everyone would be identified by the all seeing evil ball, which had once belonged to the Bishop's mother who, it was said, was a witch and used it for sorcery. The Bishop went on to say that when King John arrived on the second day, that would complete the guest list. Then all the forces of evil would be gathered at the base of the great pinnacle. On his signal, which was to be the wave of his staff, their powers along with his own would be channeled through him and thus be directed into the eye of the needle. The Bishop's menacing chuckle grew and soon gave way to a shared eruption of laughter, after whispering, "King John actually believes that once I have obtained the crown, I will simply give it to him." Their raucous laughs slowly faded down the corridors, as both men left the room to eat, drink, and celebrate their plans for success.

The evening was now firmly upon us, as the Scarlet and I arrived at Miller's Pond. There was a great deal of activity with soldiers everywhere, and as a result, we were having difficulty reaching the sayer of soothes. Then the dreaded sound of that horn was heard, and many of the soldiers quickly scurried in its direction. We were now able to move closer to the cottage, and I could see the old man sitting in a rocking chair predictably gazing into the heavens above while puffing on a long, curved pipe that emitted a curl of blue smoke, which slowly drifted upwards. Hiding within the bushes, we were now able to get within talking distance of the old man when without interrupting his gaze, he said, "Wait for me inside the cottage." The Scarlet and I took heed of his words and joined the shadows of the night while moving slowly to the rear of the cottage. My comrade and I quietly tapped three times and a robust, red-haired woman answered saying, "Come in. We have been awaiting your arrival." As we entered the woman directed us to sit by the warmth of her fire, and as we did she explained that the sooth sayer had a vision of a new "Woodargon" along with our quest ahead. The villagers had also been made aware of this vision and a renewed hope for all began to spread.

Back at the Bishop's castle, Pook's new wings had quickly started to grow, but time was running short. He tried to move the chalice toward the edge of the mantle, so it would fall while at the same time freeing him, but the cup was too heavy. Using the hair pin, he tried to wedge and maneuver his enclosure in any way that would free him, but to no avail. Pook's wings had now become fully-grown and ready for flight. He realized that his wings, especially new ones, were his most powerful attribute. With a new-found optimism, he eagerly wedged both wings under the lip of the cup while both hands slid under the pin. With all his might, he began to lift. It worked, for the chalice started to move slowly toward the edge of the mantle. His determination was becoming fruitful as both he and his domed prison slowly maneuvered their way to the mantle's edge. The cup began to waver. Finally in one last roll, it tipped and fell to the hearth below, which held many of the burning logs. Pook hovering above the fiery scene was finally free. With great speed, he disappeared through the same slatted window from which he had previously entered. The Sheriff and the Bishop had heard the commotion and quickly returned to that fated room immediately noticing the chalice lying and melting within the burning embers. The Bishop remarked, "Well, I suppose we don't have to worry about the goblin anymore."

Then the Sheriff replied, "But what if during the fall he escaped and flew away?" "Nonsense" said the Bishop, "remember I removed his wings." With smug expressions both men were now resigned to Pook's end and their sinister laughs appeared to seal their satisfaction.

PRISONERS TAKEN

Now safely inside the sooth sayer's cottage, we watched, as the old man slowly arose from his chair with the obvious intention of returning to the cottage. A moment before he could do so, two soldiers shouted to him, "You, old man! Come here!" He had no choice but to do as they asked, and as he approached one said, "There will be no star gazing tonight, old man, for not far behind, our soldiers have captured two of Robin Hood's men, and they will be passing shortly, so off the street with you."

With that the old man returned to his abode. Closing the door behind him, he said, "Did you hear the soldiers' news?" The Scarlet and I nodded with great concern, then loud voices were heard, and as they came closer, my heart sank, for we could see both John and Peter wrapped in a tangle of chains being led by several soldiers who enjoyed an occasional poke with their spears. John was very protective of Peter and turned to face their tormentors with a warning of their doomed fate. The soldiers tried to dismiss John's remarks, but their poorly attempted laughs were not convincing anyone. The leader of their group was heard to say, "The Bishop and Sheriff will be overwhelmed with joy when we lead you to the castle and we will be greatly rewarded for our deeds." The words had no sooner escaped his lips when Vargis and the Sheriff came galloping up to inspect their prize. At that moment I thought how similar both men looked to my teachers, Mr. Alritage and Mr. Travis.

"Take them to the dungeons, for we will deal with them after the day of the test," shouted Vargis as they sped off into the darkness of night looking for more human prizes. But what of Roxelena? Did she escape, or was she dead? Growing fears gnawed at my mind and guilt began to lay heavily on me; it was my decision to split up our party, yet I needed to remain hopeful for without Roxelena our quest would have little purpose.

I asked the sayer of soothes what visions he had of the great battle ahead. He replied, "I have seen a gathering like no other at the pinnacle where the struggle for power will take place, but I was not privileged to see the outcome. The vision became clouded, and I was not permitted to see what took place."

I explained our quest to the old man and told him that Roxelena, the rightful heir to the throne, was with John and Peter, but she was now missing. "We must find her, and soon," I said.

"Enough!" replied the old lady. "You must sit, rest, and eat for food helps the mind to see the way." Each of us sat silently contemplating a solution to find Roxelena and free our friends. Then the old lady called us over to her table, which was laden with food that included a chicken broth with bread along with a flagon of goat's milk. I could only nibble on the meal before me, for Roxelena became my one and only focus. We were in desperate need of a plan, but on that note we could hear someone approaching, followed by a gentle tap on the door. Quickly blowing out the large candle, I scurried to the window and noticed the shadowy figure of a small person. I slowly opened the door and to my great joy, there stood Roxelena. She had no sooner entered the cottage when, overwhelmed with relief and joy, I hugged her, perhaps a little harder than I should.

"Come be seated and have some food," said the old lady, and Roxelena smilingly complied.

"What happened, and how did you escape the soldiers?" I asked.

She replied, "The sheriff's men were everywhere, and because the moon was unkind to our position, John was seen. Realizing we could all be taken, John whispered to me, 'Stay here and keep still.' Then suddenly both Peter and John stood and ran from their hiding place in order to draw the soldiers away from me. It worked for a moment. Then, hungry for more captives, three soldiers turned back to search the spot we were in. At that moment, I raised the hood of my cape and simply wished not to be seen and it was so! Although I could see them, they could not see me. Moments later both Peter and John were captured and led away. There were just too many of them. Anyway, I waited until the way was clear before my final journey here."

We tried to console Roxelena who felt guilty for being the only one to escape, when once more we were interrupted by a faint tapping sound. There hovering at the window was Pook. The old lady opened the door exclaiming, "This cottage is as busy as a market place on a Saturday in the village." She then let Pook in with a disapproving scowl. "Don't like goblins; never did," she insisted. Pook gave her an uninterested glance trying to ignore her remarks. He quickly descended to our gathering at the table and began to relay what had happened, and what he had heard of the Bishop and Sheriff's plan. "Uh!" exclaimed Pook, "those fools think that I am dead." Then he said with pride, "It takes more than a chalice to get the better of me."

I considered Pook's words and optimistically replied, "Wait a minute! You say that King John is on his way here, and will arrive the day before the test. That's it. Don't you see? If we can lay a trap for the pretender King and kidnap him, then we will have fair exchange for the release of John and Peter." Joy began to surge as all eyes danced with anticipation.

POOK'S JOURNEY BACK

"Pook, you have done well, but more, you have proven yourself to be one of us. I have one more quest for you. Although I know you are tired and in need of sleep, you must return to the tree people with all haste and tell them to meet with us at Boar's Crossroad, for it is here that we shall kidnap the king where he must pass on his journey to the Bishop's castle." Although Pook was eager to obey the request, he seemed hesitant. I asked, "What is the matter?"

He replied, "What if the tree people do not believe me? After all, I was not the most trusted member of the woods."

"Yes!" I replied, "I see your point. I will write a note explaining everything, and it will be signed by both Roxelena and me.

"Yes," said Pook, "that's it, for everyone knows that I cannot read or write." Suddenly realizing that he had actually admitted this, he remarked, "But I could if I wanted to."

The note was written and Pook took it folding it several times before sliding it inside his belt. I remarked, "We will meet at Boar's Crossroad on the morrow's afternoon." Then before we had a chance to exchange farewells, Pook was gone.

I remarked, "For Pook there will be no rest until his message is delivered, and the same will be for us. The next two days the test will be heavy upon us, so tonight we must sleep and gather all our strength for the challenges that lay ahead."

The next morning quickly came and as predicted it came without the sun, indicating that the forces of evil were strong. It was time to prepare for the journey and the execution of our plan.

Pook was now well into his flight when suddenly and unbeknown to him, the note had slipped from his belt and fell within the lush greenery of the forest. The spunky goblin was unaware of the note's departure until almost reaching his destination. It was now Pook's task, and his alone, to convince the tree people of their rendezvous to kidnap the pretender king.

The moon again was full, and thankfully so, for it became our only source of light. Passing Miller's Pond we entered the forest on a clearly marked road that would lead us to our destination at Boar's Crossroad.

Meanwhile King John (the pretender) had entered the forest from the south. He preferred the comfort of a carriage, which was accompanied by his royal guard; there were some thirty men with fourteen riding behind the carriage, fourteen in front, and well beyond the entourage were two scouts. The king ordered his party to stop and called the captain of the guard. On his approach the king vented his anger with a tongue lashing, blaming him for the bumpy road, and demanding to know what was he going to do about it. The captain, distraught and unsure of his reply, was saved by the timely arrival of one of the scouts who came galloping up wildly waving a parchment in his hand. "I found this at the side of the road, my Lord." The king angrily snatched the note, but his eyes never left the uncertain captain.

Slowly looking down, he began to read its content. With a gasp, he exclaimed, "Those damn outlaws plan to kidnap me at Boar's Crossroad. How dare they?"

Overhearing the king, the sergeant of the guard said, "There is another route to the Bishop's castle, my Lord. It journeys through the 'dale of the dead.'"

The scout added, "But this is where Robin Hood's men were buried. It is said to be haunted by the spirit of their band."

The king replied, "Nonsense! We have the powers of evil and with it we can deal with anything." The new route was quickly whispered among the guard and their fears now became evident along with mutterings of disapproval, as they reluctantly but slowly moved on.

Our small party was now well on route to Boar's Crossroad when to our amazement we were suddenly halted in our tracks. The trail before us began to disappear and close before our very eyes, for it quickly became covered with shrub, tree, and grass. Moments later, and once again to our surprise, a new trail began to forge its way through the forest now running to the east. The Scarlet remarked, "I have heard of something like this happening once before. When Robin and the elders were traveling to meet with the treacherous Bishop, as now, their path was closed, but there was not a new one to replace it. We now know that the forest was trying to warn the band of a trap that lay ahead, but the sign was not understood, and ignoring it resulted in disaster. We should heed this sign and follow the new path."

"But what of the tree people?" I asked.

The Scarlet replied, "If we have been given the sign, then so have they." Roxelena agreed, and although I was a little reluctant, we continued on. After an hour's travel, The Scarlet exclaimed, "We are traveling towards the dale of the dead, and should be there soon."

While on route my companions told the story of our new destination and I could see their heart was heavy with the telling of it, for it was the resting place of Robin's slain comrades. We now arrived at the dale and I found it even in the darkness to be quietly beautiful and peaceful. The Scarlet needed some time, to be with his thoughts, but time alas, was running short and the tree people were not yet here, which made me wonder if they would ever get here. "Take heart," Roxelena whispered. "For what is written will be."

I responded, "Indeed, Roxelena, but I would prefer to be the author." The smile quickly ran away from my face when I saw the Scarlet scurrying toward us with a look of concern.

His now urgent voice exclaimed, "We must devise a plan even though our numbers are few."

Then that small voice that was now familiar to me said, "Now, now, don't be greedy. Surely there are enough of the king's men to go around." Then descending to our spot came Pook, and with a sigh of relief I looked up, for the trees were now alive with the tree people.

I asked, "How did you know to come here?"

Pook replied, "Well, I had lost that written message during my journey to the sanctuary, and although it took a lot to convince these leafy louts, they finally came around to my story, convinced it was too complicated even for my tiny mind. During our journey, the path before us began to disappear and a new one going east appeared showing a new path." Pook's story was indeed the same as told by the Scarlet.

A KIDNAPPING

The Scarlet said, "Many believe that the ghosts of our ancestors haunt this dale, and except for us, no one dares to travel it."

Then Roxelena replied, "So, if the king dares to travel this way…"

"Yes! That's it!" I cried, apologizing for my abrupt interruption, but the excitement of revelation got the better of me. "Gather round for this will be our plan. Here beside the road, we will make a mock grave site. I shall be in that grave, except for my head and one hand, and in it I will have my flashlight. As the kings men approach, I will turn it first on me, then shine it upward toward this tree where there will be a score of tree people whaling, shaking, and moving all about."

Pook and the others were puzzled and asked, "What is a flashlight?" My explanation seemed to mean little to them until I gave a demonstration. Pook was now totally entranced by its magic and asked if he too could make the magic. I obliged him only for a moment for preparations were in need of making, and so I closed by simply asking them to trust my gadget and me.

The Scarlet protested, "But what about the scouts? There are always scouts when traveling these woods."

I replied, "We shall let them ride past where four of our tree people shall set a trip rope. At the chosen spot at the point of their fall, a camouflaged net will be laid so that for a while, they will become a guest of our friend the tree."

The Scarlet exclaimed, "What if our plan fails?"

I responded, "We will not do battle with the soldiers, for we trespass on hallowed ground. If the plan goes awry, everyone must vanish into the darkness of the forest, and we shall all meet at Miller's Pond." Nodding heads sealed the end of our discussion and everyone moved to their position.

Almost an hour had passed with still no sign of the king, then word came that he and his party were not far away, and soon he would enter our position. We later discovered that their delay was due to the king stopping his entourage every fifteen minutes so he could continue to blame and berate the captain for his bumpy ride.

The scouts now cautiously entered our location and warily rode by. Then as if escaping an unseen force, they hurriedly galloped past the dale thinking they were well out of any dangers. To their surprise, upon entering the chosen place of their capture, they fell victim and succumbed to their fate. Moments later the king's party approached as the scouts cries could be heard in the distance, which unnerved the advancing soldiers. At that exact moment our plan went into action. Its timing and execution was a great success, for as planned that beam of light shone only on my head protruding from the mock grave, then upward to the tree, which now became alive with the tree people wailing and shaking. All the soldiers ahead of the carriage were now aghast at the sights before them. Horses reared and men cried in fear as bedlam reined all about. Moments later they frantically turned and rode back past the royal carriage as the king shook his fists at their cowardly withdrawal. It appeared that the rear guard took heed and followed their retreating comrades. Suddenly the pretender king was now all alone, and as he arrogantly exited the carriage, I noticed that there was a definite similarity to my school headmaster, for he was a man in his fifties, short in stature, and, of course, overdressed. His defiance erupted in my direction as he said, "Do you know who I am, you peasant dogs?" He then began to call on the powers of darkness to strike me down.

In turn I simply held up the small wooden cross, and said, "In the name of Christianity be gone all evil, for you are not welcome here."

Moments later smoke began to appear from the king's mouth, and he cried "Please stop it; I'm in great pain." With that, one of the tree people approached and threw a flagon of water over his head, which cooled his arrogant manner and dampened his spirits.

Then to our surprise, just as we were about to lead him away, several of the rear guard soldiers who had been hiding in the bushes, emerged as one said, "You did not trick us." They came forward menacingly with swords in hand prepared to do their worst. We now had no choice but to defend ourselves, but the soldiers advance came to an abrupt halt, for suddenly out of the calm still of the night there appeared from behind us, ghostly apparitions which drifted around and through where we were standing. We soon discovered they were the dead elders led by Robin who gave a cheeky wink in my direction. They moved menacingly towards the king's men, and if the soldiers were not frightened before, they certainly were now. Not long after, their cries could be heard almost a mile away as they quickly disappeared into the thick darkness of the forest. Cheers of joy resounded as our smiling, ghostly comrades retreated from whence they came.

The Scarlet exclaimed, "Even in death, our ancestors are with us." A great satisfaction mixed with pride was written on everyone's face. The king, noticeably shaken by what he had seen, was now ours to bargain with. As we departed, a gentle rain began to fall, which seemed to soothe the beating of my heart, and with it the tensions of the day began to dissolve. I quietly gave my thanks to our friend, the forest, which showed us the sign and the way ahead, and, of course, to Robin and his loyal band for watching over us.

The kidnapping

The Exchange

The two captured scouts would now become our couriers, and they would carry the news of our prize to the Bishop. A letter was written explaining our plan: the king would be exchanged along with the release of our friends, Peter and John. If any harm had come to them, the same fate would, indeed, befall the pretender king. Our meeting would take place as the cock crows at Miller's Pond — we on the forest side and the Bishop's party on the village side. Rowboats would be placed on both sides and at the given signal, one person rowing would accompany the prisoners. We now departed for Miller's Pond with a newfound optimism. From above I noticed a hawk that appeared to be following. He would intermittently fly low to observe our captured prize and finally decided to express his opinion with the release of a "bowel bomb," which found its target as our prisoner looked up. Satisfied with the completion of his task the hawk then departed. On our arrival to the pond, a small party continued on and escorted the scouts through the village and up to the castle, watching as the pair entered the castle's keep. Minutes later the Bishop's exploding anger could be heard even in the village, and I quietly wondered what fate would befall the two scouts who had delivered the news.

Vargis furiously called for the council of sorcerers, creatures of all shape and size, who were attending the festival of darkness. Upon their arrival to the great hall, they were accompanied by a lingering foul odor that persistently followed their presence. The Bishop was dressed in red from head to foot, and he looked every part the conniving devil that he was. He now entered the hall displaying that familiar imperious look, which I suspect was enhanced for the benefit of the masses. The Sheriff, like a lap dog, was of course not far behind. Vargis ordered everyone to be seated, and they nervously complied, leaning on his every word. The Bishop continued, "You know the plan for the morrow, and I expect all of you to play your part in it." He searched all eyes for any signs of weakness. "Now for the business of the day: Your king has been abducted by this peasant rabble, and they are asking for an exchange of prisoners at Miller's Pond, where boats on either side will be dispersed along with the prisoners. I will devise a military plan to deal with these dogs, but I expect you to come up with a way of disposing of the prisoners. I will return within the hour for your suggestion and be sure it is to my liking, or else!"

The Bishop's party quickly left the hall to the sound of mutterings and scheming, which now filled the air. An hour had passed and the Bishop promptly returned impatiently demanding to know of their plan. A small hunched creature emerged from the congregation and said, "Sire, if this exchange is to take place on yonder pond, we can create a new but unwanted resident within its depths. It will attack and devour all in that boat which contains a raw cut of meat. Of course, that cut of meat will be placed in our enemy's boat, and the prisoners will be blindfolded, so the game shall not be given away."

The Bishop was now uncommonly beside himself with joy, and replied, "Excellent! Excellent! And my soldiers will finish off the rest of those dogs. Then on the morrow, the day of success will be ours and ours alone." The great hall, which carried that noticeable odor, had now grown to become a foul stench as excitement within its ranks grew.

Back at Miller's Pond we settled in for the evening. Again the king with the return of that familiar arrogance began his barrage of complaints: The night air was too cold; the ground was too hard for sleeping on; and, where was the grand meal that he was accustomed to? Roxelena as did the rest of us became bored with his endless whining complaints, so she removed some silk scarves from his attire and with them, tied and gagged him.

The morning dew arrived while the darkness as predicted stubbornly refused to leave, and all was made official by the crowing of the cock that must have been a little confused with the lack of early morning light, yet his instinctive clock knew the truth. Now gathered at the pond a blanket of fog could be seen as it slowly drifted back across its sparkling waters to find a resting place in a nearby marsh. It was as if the stage had been set and the curtain was raised to show the oncoming scene. Knowing full well of the Bishop's treacherous ways, we positioned lit torches to surround the pond, while the tree people were located within the bushes. We waited for the Bishop's party to arrive, and there in the distance we could see them. The Bishop and the Sheriff were accompanied by the sorcerers. The Sheriff was happy to lead their parade pulling John and Peter behind bound in those heavy, foreboding chains. They were now blindfolded and attended by some 70 soldiers, all armed with long bows. This made me suspicious, for as my history lessons reminded me, Norman soldiers usually preferred and used crossbows. Vargis and his party finally arrived at the pond accompanied by their screaming threats that we would all be dead before the day was done. The scene was set, and prisoners on both sides were put in small boats that would be rowed by their own man. All was ready as we awaited the signal from a burning torch.

Roxelena exclaimed, "Beware their treacherous ways for as an enemy they posses no chivalry."

I nodded my agreement with her and remarked, "Fear not, Roxelena, for I am prepared for the evil ways of Vargis." With that, the burning torch was waved and both boats slowly left their birth with each holding a lit beacon so we could see its progress. Again more insults were hurled by the king as his boat slowly passed that of our comrades, and with the journey almost two thirds of its way done, we could see the Sheriff's men preparing for conflict as I had suspected. They raised their long bows each with burning arrows aimed at us. I asked all to be prepared for the inevitable onslaught. As their arrows were released, I raised my staff on high and cried, "Change their fiery destination to one who needs to be cleansed." Magically in mid air the shafted barrage indeed changed their intended route as if drawn by an invisible force, and now journeyed toward the king's boat. Plunging into the middle of the craft, all grouped within a two-foot diameter, they created a large hole, which gave way to the oncoming water. The water quickly put out their flames, and soon thereafter the boat began to sink. Roxelena and I noticed the waters of the pond had become agitated and realized that something was amiss. Suddenly the pond's surface was broken by the site of a large sea monster. It loomed and hovered above the pond preparing to strike its intended victims, so at that moment I again raised my staff on high and ordered a retreat to its creator. The creature now began its journey to the opposite side of the pond where the king and his rower had been forced into the cold, murky waters a few yards from shore. The creature briefly appeared devouring the small boat as both the rower and the king staggered ashore. The serpent's appetite had been stirred for more than a mere boat, but his meal would not be realized, for the Bishop was now disgusted with the turn of events and used his powers to be rid of the monster. As it dissolved into thin air so did its threat.

Vargis cried, "Who among you dares to interfere with my will?"

A deafening silence was broken by the response, "I am Robert also know as the 'Woodargon' of this forest, and be it known, Vargis, that your days of tyranny in this land will soon be at an end."

The soldiers' respectful silence was again broken by the king who angrily discharged more insults as he floundered on land looking like a drowned rat. In his retreat, he cried, "You'll pay for this you, Saxon dogs." Returning to the castle, they and their mutterings disappeared into the night. The Bishop could be heard chastising all for their incompetence. John and Peter now released from their chains were none the worse for wear except for some minor wounds received by the guards spears, for which Roxelena was happy to treat. Both were overjoyed to once again being back in our company and raring to be of use for our cause.

An exhange of prisoners

The Pinnacle

Our foe had no sooner entered the castle when the silence of the night was loudly broken as the villagers clumsily spilled into the street cheering and chanting, "Woodargon, Woodargon…" They joyously came toward us led by the sayer of soothes along with his wife. On their arrival we noticed that they had brought food and merriment, exclaiming, "We have not seen a victory such as this for many years." Meanwhile back in the shadows of the castle, the pretender king spoke of all he had seen and heard including the news of Roxelena, the true heir to the throne. He also talked of the 'Woodargon' who wielded great powers.

Vargis, seemingly uninterested in this news, appeared as always to be drowning in his own vanity and closed the discussion by saying, "No matter. These peasants are no match for the powers within these walls."

Back at Miller's Pond the sayer of soothes remarked with a serious tone, "We must be prepared for the morrow for all will need to take heart. The test of power and your challenge to defeat Vargis and his villainous band will be great." Continuing, the old man said, "Let us sit and talk of the pinnacle." So we all gathered around the fire's hypnotic, dancing flames. The elder resumed, "The mighty rock known as the 'pinnacle' holds the royal needle and the 'walk of doom' must be taken to claim the crown of this kingdom. It is located firmly above the needles eye."

Then John Little added that no one had ever completed the deadly journey, for during the treacherous walk along its shaft, the eye becomes aware of its trespasser and opens with a mighty wind, which stirs from within it. All who have attempted the walk have fallen to their deaths on the rocks below. Only one has cheated this fate; it was Vargis. Like the others, the mighty wind dislodged his footing from the needles shaft, but his newly created wings allowed a safe landing below. It is rumored that the needle's eye is that of King Richard, and he protects the crown until the day its rightful heir will claim it.

The Scarlet intervened to say, "For a safe journey to the crown, the needle's eye must be closed, and you, Roxelena, must take that walk of doom."

Roxelena proudly replied, "I will take the walk of doom, for it is my destiny to do so."

Still curious I asked, "Tell me more of the pinnacle and its surrounding area."

John slowly began to speak with a deliberate and serious purpose. "The pinnacle is a mighty rock that reaches up to the stars. Near its summit is the royal needle, which is embedded within it. Along its shaft a walk of thirty feet will take you to its end, where both the eye and the crown are located. Below, lay the jagged rocks of the dead where many a creature has lost its life. Around the base of the pinnacle for a circle of a mile, nothing grows and the forest stops abruptly at that point. There you will see a deformed and dying oak tree. It was once the largest and most beautiful tree in all of England, but Vargis, after his failed attempt to retrieve the crown, went into a fit of temper and ordered the mighty tree's death. The great oak was too large to cut down, but typical of his cruelty, he ordered all its branches to be removed one by one, so that it would die slowly. It was done, but for one small branch. Although the tree looks dead, it barely clings to life supporting its one and only branch."

At that moment no more words were necessary, for each one of us were now left with our own thoughts about what was said, the task ahead, and what might be.

My mind considered the turn of events for the morrow, but its lingering concern was for Roxelena. She was a young girl slight of frame but large in spirit. Her task ahead was monumental. Then a vision of Robin appeared reminding me of his last words, "Be not afraid. Trust your heart, for mine is with all of you." With that I felt a renewed faith both in us and our cause.

The night air was cool and clear. As I looked into the sleeping heavens, a shooting star slashed across, and all things now seemed right under God's cloak of darkness. Roxelena had now approached and sat down beside me, having seen the earlier concern my face had been wearing. She said, "Fear not, Woodargon, for our cause is just and the outcome for the morrow is now truly written." I smiled at her as she snuggled closer for warmth and I thought, *yes, this time it truly is.* With curiosity Roxelena then asked, "Tell me of your world; are you happy living in it?"

A smile emerged as I replied, "My world is filled with many wondrous things where some travel by horseless carriages, and we speak into a machine called a telephone, which allows a two-way conversation with many miles between the speakers. Yes, I am happy to be living in my world for it is the time where I belong. Yet I grow to also love this world for those I have come to care for and admire — for this is a time of honor and chivalrous deeds when man must seek the truth within his own heart." I looked longingly into her eyes. "In this world I have discovered that nature is also truly a wondrous thing." Our heads began to droop as a yawn was exchanged and with that, sleep swept over us to give respite from all burdens of the day. The morrow's reckoning would be with us soon enough.

Once again, proof of the morning arrived with the distant crowing of the morning bird that defiantly would not be deterred from his duty. I awoke from a contented slumber and immediately called a meeting with Peter, John, Scarlet, Roxelena, and Pook. The sayer of soothes intervened to inform us that he and the villagers wished to be included in our plans, for without victory their lives would not be worth living. With a placid blink, I considered his request, and then finally gave an approving nod, which could not disguise that lurking smile now emerging on his face.

All were now assembled as they sat and listened with deep interest to the plan that was about to unfold. After careful considerations, I began, "We shall journey to the pinnacle in three groups. The tree people led by the Scarlet will enter from the south. The villagers will enter from the west, and we will arrive from the east. But remember this, you must stay hidden, and no one is to go beyond the edge of the forest. To finalize my strategy, I will again need the eyes and ears of Pook."

Standing erect with chest popping, Pook asked, "Will I get a medal for all my deeds?"

I replied, "Well, of course, Pook, perhaps two, but only if you are successful on this last mission. You are to fly to the pinnacle some five leagues away and review their force and position along with any other information you can gather. Remember, you must be back no later than mid-day."

Pook replied, "Fear not, for I will do my part. Oh, and by the way," insisted Pook with a serious tone, "be sure not to make the medals too heavy, for they may impede my flying." With that, he was gone.

Pook soon arrived at the pinnacle to a sight that even he was in awe of, for at the base of the great rock were the sorcerers attended by Vargis and his entourage. Outside and surrounding them, were four large catapults aimed at the royal needle and anyone who may attempt the "walk of doom." Again beyond and surrounding their position were some two-hundred soldiers protecting all within. He also noticed that the step path leading up the face of the pinnacle was guarded by some thirty soldiers spaced at ten-yard intervals. It appeared that Vargis had thought of everything. Pook now decided to descend to a spot close to the Bishop's tent. In doing so, he overheard Vargis talking to his lieutenants, emphasizing that, when the time was right, all their firepower must be directed to the eye of the needle. Then, turning to a handful of sorcerers, he insisted that when he was in a position to again take that fateful journey, their collective powers along with his own would surely end the life of the needle's eye. Pook realized he now had enough information for 'Woodargon,' and so he began his retreat when suddenly some of the Sheriff's soldiers spotted him and a flurry of arrows were released in Pook's direction. One appeared to catch him in the neck, and with a scream of pain, he awkwardly but swiftly fell just within the edge of the forest. Soldiers were now quickly dispatched to find him.

Back at Miller's Pond, weapons were being dispensed and preparations for battle were in the making. It was getting close to mid-day, and Pook was not to be seen. A final meeting had to take place, but without Pook's report, it would mean little. The time of his return had now passed, and I dared not delay any longer. We gathered and began to discuss our strategy when a voice was heard, “Look! It’s Pook!” He now came into view hovering into camp with great difficulty, for he had indeed been wounded with a large gash to the neck, and consequently he had lost much blood.

“Come, Pook. Lie down here,” I insisted.

“No!” he whispered, “time is running short, and there is much to be said.” In a quiet voice, Pook went into detail of all he had seen and heard. When finished, he looked weak and tired.

At that moment the sayer of soothes’s wife came forward now showing a respectful eye towards Pook and insisted, “Give him to me. I shall care for him at my cottage.”

THE BATTLE PLAN

I pondered on what Pook had seen, which now confirmed our course of action, explaining to all within earshot that there was a way that our plan may succeed if we all worked together. Now turning to the sayer of soothes, I asked, "How many sheep's horns can you gather?"

With a quizzical look, he replied, "Seven or eight."

"Good," I answered. "Quickly get them, and give three to the tree people, and two for us, then you and the villagers will keep the rest. When we all arrive at the pinnacle but still within the forest, the village people will give the first signal of the horn. Each group will respond with a single blow on their horn to show we have all arrived. Then many hundreds of torches must be lit after which all the horns must be blown, and a loud human voice should be heard to make the soldiers believe that there are great hordes of men. It should confuse the enemy to think that they are surrounded by a mighty force." Turning to Roxelena, I rested my hand on her shoulder and said, "You must, with the aid of your cloak, pass the guards on your journey up the pinnacle. When you have reached the royal needle, show yourself for but a moment. When I have seen you, I will send a second arrow, and that will be the signal for the tree people to release their flaming, oil-soaked arrows, which will find their destination at the four wooden catapults. The ensuing black smoke will hide the needle from all the soldiers. I will climb to the top of that dying oak tree so I may have a clear view of you, Roxelena, and the royal needle. When you see me waving my staff that will be the moment to begin your walk while I focus all my powers against Vargis and the sorcerers."

Roxelena displayed a widening smile and with admiring eyes, she said, "It's a fine plan, Woodargon."

Scarlet added with excitement, "Fine! It's a great plan." Quickly realizing his impertinence, he returned an apologetic glance toward Roxelena. A renewed optimism now flowed through the ranks, and all were eager to put the plan to its test. Again as we prepared to depart, there were rumblings within the ground, which grew then slowly subsided, and with them we were reminded of the impending doom.

Together we all departed for the pinnacle in three groups eventually each separating to travel his or her own route. The day's air was heavy with anticipation of what would be, and the moon was full giving off a brightness as if to make up for the loss of the sun's light. As I watched and thought about each member of our group, a smile began to take command of my face for I was truly among friends.

There was Peter, my dearest friend, who with no complaint had stayed with me through thick and thin, both now and before we came into this world. We had a natural understanding and deep respect for each other; even brothers could not have been closer than Peter and I. He was a young man always quick to help without judgments.

Then John Little, a giant of a man, with truth and honor, who like Robin cared about the world we lived in. Even as an older man he is still prepared to fight the good fight. John is a man of few spoken words and prefers to walk the walk with as little talk as possible, and yet I understood this man better than most.

The Scarlet is a young man that any father would be proud of, for he is unafraid of all the dangers that persist. Unlike John Little, the Scarlet is a man of many words, all spoken from the heart. He is always eager to taste what the world has to offer, as is his right.

And, of course, Roxelena, a maiden of great beauty, which could not be measured. More than that, I respected her fearless drive for fairness and truth, and I knew it would have been easy for me to fall in love with her. She was truly a queen beyond her birthright, a wise leader, and an example for us all. Truly my thoughts would often linger on the fair Roxelena.

I knew that each would do their part in this struggle, and that persistent smile on my face would not leave until the day's impending events would make it.

In the distance I could see the pinnacle. It was exactly as my mind had pictured. Then as we came closer, I realized that it was even bigger than I had first thought. Suddenly the ground beneath our feet began to give way to those rumblings, again as a reminder of what was to come.

As foretold we came upon the roadblock, which consisted of two sorcerers and around a dozen soldiers. "Halt!" yelled their captain as predictably the evil ball revealed our identity. Just as the officer was about to advance on us, I held up my staff and asked that they be frozen in time until the end of our conflict, and so it was. Moving on past the still figures, we finally reached our destination at the edge of the forest that encircled the great pinnacle. There we got our first overwhelming glimpse of the site and our enemy, but still remained confident in our plan and its element of surprise. We now waited until the first signal was to be given. Peter approached and insisted, "I wouldn't have missed this for anything. Fear not, Robert, for our cause is just, and we will win the day." I slowly nodded my agreement and returned his words with a thank you and a hug.

Then I noticed Roxelena sitting alone with her thoughts of what was soon to be. I attended her trying to reassure and give comfort, but it seemed that none was necessary for she looked longingly into my eyes and with a determined voice said, "I will do my part this day, for I do not fear the evil of man." At that moment reaching into my pocket that small wooden cross was retrieved and I placed it around her neck murmuring, "You are truly the queen of this realm. May this cross protect you from all harm."

She smiled and gave a kiss to my cheek replying, "If we are victorious, will you stay in our world?"

I disappointingly replied, "I cannot, fair Roxelena, for my destiny forbids it." A moment of disappointment was shared.

The Pinnacle

THE CONFLICT

We were interrupted by the first signal and with it Roxelena squeezed my hand. Again with that determined look of resolve that I had seen so often, she said, “It is the moment of truth.” Then, she quickly disappeared into the night. At that same moment all the horns were intermittently sounding in unison along with a great human noise. Hundreds of torches were lit, and the surrounding forest came alive with noise and light. The soldiers were now visibly shaken by what they thought was a large army surrounding them. I made my way a short distance to the chosen tree and on my arrival noticed the cruel devastation imposed upon it by Vargis. I placed my staff on its trunk and slowly the once mighty tree began to revitalize with new branches and foliage, quickly growing to its former greatness. The soldiers also noticed the trees rebirth, which added to their state of confusion and fear. From the forest side I now climbed the tree’s height with ease, and the second signal was made. On queue, the Scarlet and the tree people dispensed of their burning arrows aimed toward the catapults. Bedlam reined all about the soldiers for they still had not seen their foe, which appeared to make their fears even greater. It finally became more than they could bear and one by one they began to throw their arms to the ground in surrender.

I had now reached the tree’s summit and soon realized that although I could see the needle along with that brief glimpse of

Roxelena, I could not see Vargis and his assorted villains below because of that thick, rising, black smoke. How would I protect Roxelena when I couldn't see the enemy? My fears began to grow as she now became visible and prepared to take the walk of doom. Her cloak would no longer protect her during the walk, for she needed to be seen to take both the journey and the crown at its end. Roxelena now descended the granite steps to the shaft of the royal needle and with her head held erect, she slowly stepped upon it and began her walk. On seeing her, Vargis was outraged that she would dare to do this against his will, and so he began to summon all the powers of the sorcerers along with his own. I could see Roxelena holding that small wooden cross before her as she took each careful step along the narrow shaft. She had walked half way along the needle when the evil powers of Vargis and the sorcerers could now be seen. Vargis was outraged at her boldness. How dare this child oppose his will? His anger turned into the release of small balls of fire, which were now discharged, and began to fly toward her. At first they were well wide of their target but getting noticeably closer with each projectile. I had to do something, so I raised my staff and pointed it toward the eye of the needle, which had now opened without the usually accompanying wind. I felt all the power of the staff release and enter the needle's eye with the hope it would now become the single source of our power. Moments later, a great shaft of white light emerged from the eye. For a moment it appeared that daylight had returned. Its beam shone down on all the scheming throng below, and it seemed that a moment in time was held with a mist that had descended to hide any movement from their location. Now it became safe for Roxelena to complete the walk of doom. As she successfully reached her destination, she kneeled before the royal crown, slowly lifting it from its perch, while the needle's eye appeared to keep a vigil. The darkness of night glowed to a golden sunset and on her return walk Roxelena could see the activities below, for as the mist cleared. What were once the evil ones had become transformed into small, squealing, black pigs all in a state of utter confusion running in endless circles. One pig stood out from the rest for he had a red patch on his chest, and it became obvious what his former identity was.

Cheers of victory echoed for miles around, and even the captured soldiers seemed to be relieved that they now had a true and benevolent leader.

The lingering mist slowly parted to show Roxelena descending from the pinnacle with her just prize. As she turned back for one last look at the needle and its eye, she saw what she thought was a wink. In return she gave a smiling wink back, a fitting farewell to a father she had never known. We all ran to our brave queen falling to our knees in homage. She responded, "Rise my friends and subjects for our victory was well earned by all." She slowly moved towards me, and while I was still on my knees, she said, "Rise, Woodargon, for 'tis you that we should all be paying homage to."

Red-faced and unsure, I replied, "It was my destiny your highness, for I did no more than anyone else here."

She responded, "It may have been your destiny, but without your plan that carried both wisdom and bravery, we would not have succeeded — and all without the loss of a single life."

The following morning came quickly, and we stirred to the sound of birds accompanied by a magnificent dawn that must have been such as the first man had seen, but the joy of its sight was interrupted by rumblings from beneath, which now grew to become a great earthquake. The ground began to tremble as we all fell down to it, and from above we could see the violent shaking had now dislodged the needle from its holder. Soon after, it fell to the deadly rocks below, and its final resting place for its purpose was now at an end. We knew that with this violent earthquake, the sanctuary would be no more.

Concerned for Pook I was anxious to return to the village. Our convoy stretched for almost a league led by the village people, the tree people, our own party, and trailing were the soldiers followed by that newly created pig family, snorting and squealing with every step, each struggling for a position in front of their column. We noticed that the pig with the red patch on his chest was constantly pushed and kept to the very rear of their number.

Entering the village we approached the sayer of soothes's cottage. Before I reached the door, it opened swiftly before me. Upon our entry the old lady appeared and greeted us with a sigh of relief and a hug that would make a mere mortal beg for mercy. I asked, "What of Pook?" No sooner had the words left my lips, than out from nowhere darted Pook wearing a large bandage wrapped around his neck and head allowing only his long ears the freedom from that upper mummified bondage.

With great excitement he said, "I knew it; I knew it! The day is ours, and don't forget, you owe me a medal."

No! Two medals!" I replied. "Yes, Pook, and you shall have them, for they are well earned, but first you must rest until you are well enough to travel. We must continue on to the sanctuary to see what devastation has befallen it." Then suddenly entering our location came half a dozen assorted goblins of all age and size. With pride Pook introduced his family to us.

"This is my sister, Sook, my brother, Mook and my mother and father, Kook and Zook." He added, "The world of goblins has heard of our great feats especially mine, so in turn they have invited me to return home."

The day had truly ended well, and I gave my thanks to Pook along with a gift of my flashlight. He remembered its magic from the dale of the dead and eagerly thanked me in return. We then waved our goodbyes as he and his brother carried off their prize.

The soldiers were now informed that in our absence the sayer of soothes would be in charge. In turn their captain, who now appeared relieved of his previous tormentor, gladly nodded his understanding. It seemed that the new dawn had brought with it a new day in the lives of all these people, and their freedom overflowed with a joy I'm sure they had not known before.

Our Final Journey

Again my concerns began to calm with our travels through the woodland, for as before it displayed that same silent and reassuring beauty that I had come to know so well. This was perhaps our final journey now steered toward the sanctuary and with it I feared the worst. What had become of our beautiful safe haven? We would know soon enough. It was getting late in the day yet the sun refused to run and hide, almost as if it were making up for lost time. On the final leg of our trip, we were becoming uncertain and nervous at what may lay ahead. Then there, over the last hill was our destination. We cautiously reached its summit and the sight now before us was more than we could bear, for my breath was taken from me without permission. The sanctuary had risen to the world above in all its perfect glory, and what once appeared below was now before us, basking in all the splendor of the day's golden hours. Great joy was the order of the day and queen Roxelena announced that from this place she would rule her kingdom.

Peter turned to me and whispered, "Robert, is it not the time of our departure?"

I nodded with a look of remorse, for our destiny had truly been fulfilled and it was time to return to our own place and time. I turned to all assembled and with sadness said, "The day is late but early on the morrow we must depart, for the world of our time beckons."

Then with knitted brow, the Scarlet replied, "But you are still the Woodargon and guardian of our world. You must stay and protect us and this place."

"Yes!" I replied, "I am your Woodargon, but our destinies have been fulfilled. Remember Robin's words: 'Be not afraid and trust your heart, for mine is with all of you.' Now, you have a strong and just queen to rule this kingdom, and remember, each one of you has a greater knowledge and courage to fight the evils of you're world."

Roxelena announced, "Tonight we shall celebrate and make merry." But our attempts to do so failed miserably. We were all so tired that, one by one, we fell into a contented and well deserved sleep. The youth of morning arrived with the promise of a new and peaceful world, and so it would be. It was time to put on our own clothes. I also noticed that the tree people were no longer dressed in their usual camouflage but appeared as they should. Now my lingering thoughts gave way to words of farewell. I gave John Little and the Scarlet a farewell hug, and thanked each for their loyalty and support.

The Scarlet replied, "We shall never forget you." In turn their respectfully bowed heads were enough and needed no further words.

I approached Queen Roxelena and kneeled to give homage saying, "With you now ruler of this land, I have no fear for its future, for I know it will prosper as never before." A persistent silence was interrupted by my words of farewell, which struggled to escape my lips. "Goodbye, fair Roxelena, and always know that the heart of a true queen beats with the heart of her people. May peace descend upon you all with a sweet and tender grace, and may joy and hope take to wing to find that special place within. Don't forget Pook's medals, for he well deserves them. Live long and be happy, great Queen."

Once more with tears welling to spill their banks, Roxelena gently pulled me to my feet and kissed me on the lips saying, "You are truly the greatest Woodargon of this land." "We thank you for fulfilling your destiny."

With hesitation Peter and I said a heartfelt final goodbye to everyone, and we slowly walked away. Turning for one last wave a mist descended, and we lost site of them and the sanctuary almost as if it were a dream. Peter turned to me and asked, "How will we find our way home?"

I replied, "Fate brought us here, and fate will surely return us." Then ahead we saw that familiar grave site as it appeared on our first sighting, so we knew that we had now returned to our own place and time. We said our farewells to Robin with the promise of a visit once a year, and then we walked on, for not far ahead was that familiar field. From there we descended the hill and soon found that same path, which led to the gully where our two-wheeled steeds were still waiting. I became aware of something in my jacket pocket and reaching into it, I discovered and retrieved the small wooden cross, which I had previously given to Roxelena. She must have quietly returned it without my knowing. It would become more than a symbol of our faith for I would treasure it above and beyond all possessions. Once again, I would be late in getting home and strangely relished the thought of it. Peter and I made a pact and swore that on this day, July the 25th, we would celebrate our amazing journey until the day of our deaths. For Peter, that celebration has now come to an end, and I miss him dearly, for he was not only a true friend but more like the brother I never had. We shared much from early childhood all through the years. Together Peter and I were privileged to be part of a great adventure that few would ever know of.

Seven years later I was able to purchase five acres of land surrounding and including our treasured site, explaining to its recent owner that this spot had become a favorite picnic area for my family and me, which indeed it had. As a farmer the woodland was of no interest to him and he appeared grateful to have made a small profit on its sale.

I continue to pursue my creative abilities, painting the beauty of this world, especially the woodlands, which provide an endless joy, even though my sight is no longer what it used to be.

Robin's grave site is still hidden in that special place within the forest. Physically I can no longer visit it, yet I know the grave site remains, untouched and unseen. Only those who understand its secrets are privileged to see it, and although the woodland has been reduced for the expansion of mankind and his technologies, that historic site still clings to its chosen place.

Now, in my advancing years, I am surrounded with the comfort of my family and a plethora of memories. Recently my grandson, Stephen, who is now sixteen, strangely began to show the sign of a birthmark that was not there before. It is identical in shape and location to my own yet its presence baffles me.

Printed in the United States
31279LVS00002B/252

9 781413 733310